DON'T MISS A SINGLE
KENT MONTANA ADVENTURE!

Kent Montana and the Really Ugly Thing from Mars
IT is big. IT is ugly. IT has a heat ray and a nasty
disposition. IT is, in short, the worst thing to happen
to New Jersey since the last election.

Kent Montana and the Reasonably Invisible Man
A mad scientist has discovered the secret of (temporary) invisibility. He's not planning to sneak into
the movies, either. He's mad, remember? He wants
revenge!

Kent Montana and the Once and Future Thing
Down on the bayou, a man-eating she-beast is look-
ing for a little affection. Or possibly . . . commitment.
And guess who the swamp-mistress has fallen for?

THE MARK OF
THE MODERATELY
VICIOUS VAMPIRE

LIONEL FENN

ACE BOOKS, NEW YORK

This book is an Ace original edition,
and has never been previously published.

THE MARK OF THE MODERATELY VICIOUS VAMPIRE

An Ace Book / published by arrangement with
the author

PRINTING HISTORY
Ace edition / May 1992

ISBN: 0-441-51970-9

Ace Books are published by The Berkley Publishing Group,
200 Madison Avenue, New York, New York 10016.
The name "ACE" and the "A" logo
are trademarks belonging to Charter Communications, Inc.

PRINTED IN THE UNITED STATES OF AMERICA

10 9 8 7 6 5 4 3 2 1

It is a proven fact that the creatures depicted within this film do not now, nor have they ever existed, to the absolute knowledge of the director and the writer.

It is also a proven fact that, in days of old, absolute knowledge asserted that the world was flat, kings were anointed by the direct hand of God, and Australians spent their whole lives standing on their heads.

Therefore, it is my studied opinion that knowledge is what you make of it, including the doilies on the back of your aunt's sofa and which are hell to get the hair grease out of.

—Timothy Boggs
  (younger brother of Lionel Fenn, who still hasn't sold his first book but not to worry because he has a real job now, even if he'd rather be writing his second book in the hopes that his first book will sell for a million dollars so that he doesn't have to write his second book, or one of these stupid introduction things either)

- I -

Damsel In Distress, With Wolf

✦ 1 ✦

The small but not provincial about it coastal community of Assyria, in Maine, had never quite seen the like of it before.

Without warning, from all points of the horizon, massive dark clouds rose above the land and crawled up from the sea to swallow the sky and bring the night early. No lightning. No thunder. Not a single touch of wind.

Just the clouds.

And the silence.

All of which ended a few hours later when a pretty vicious bolt of lightning fractured the midnight sky.

Suddenly there were winds that lifted waves so high, it seemed as if the ocean itself were rising from its bed; winds so strong that doors and windows rattled in their frames, trees were stripped of their leaves, and the leaves themselves flew like claw-shaped hail. The rain that followed flooded every street and filled every drain almost instantly, washed gravel from driveways and pounded flowers into the mud, found cracks in roofs and splits in walls and spat into houses before it could be stopped.

The lightning.

A tree in the forest exploded at its touch, another became a torch short-lived in the deluge; a mast on a fishing vessel was shattered to splinters, each splinter an ember that flared briefly in the dark; a massive boulder on the high rocky headland was split in half, and half again; and when it didn't strike the ground, the lightning seemed to strike the water, tease it, torment it, ripping the black apart and mending it again in seconds.

Nothing moved but the wind and rain.

Nothing, that is, save a solitary boat, exposed and helpless on the water.

Its proud, surf-battered prow, despite the storm's best attempts to turn it, remained steadfastly aimed toward the distant shoreline, splitting the waves where it couldn't ride them, riding the waves when it could ever closer to the beach below the town. Thunder snarled at it, the wind bellowed at it, lightning tried and failed a hundred times to strike it, but still the boat moved onward.

A curious boat.

A lonely boat.

It was, in fact, a purple dinghy.

No one worked the oars, which twisted and turned aimlessly; no one sat defiantly at the rudder, which had long ago been wrenched from its mooring; no one stood amidships, bravely bailing with his bare bloody hands and screaming defiant curses at the elements.

It was empty.

Almost.

For, snugly wedged beneath the fore and aft plank seats, was an unadorned oblong crate just over six feet long. The ocean charged over the gunwales, the rain pounded on its top, but the curious cargo did not tremble, neither did it shift.

The beach drew nearer.

The purple dinghy labored on.

Impossibly, the lightning doubled, and doubled again, and the beleaguered craft was driven slightly southward, away from the sodden sandy beach toward a section of the shore where large rocks and small boulders hunched with kelp against the elements.

The left oar snapped and whirled away into the dark.

The dinghy spun crazily across the crest of a wave, and the right oar snapped as well.

A second wave drove the battered vessel closer, a third even more, and a fourth, huge, roaring leviathan mother of a curl lifted it clear of the sand and sent it crashing among the rocks where its prow was severely blunted, its keel split, and the oblong crate burst through the planks and was flung end over end between the two largest boulders.

When it landed, a jagged crack appeared along its top.

When a distant flare of blue-white briefly illuminated the night a few minutes later, the crack had widened.

When thunder finally arrived, the top was gone.

The mysterious crate was empty.

But the beach was not deserted.

Not far from the boulders and rocks and quivering kelp, a shadow made its way erratically across the beach, squishing a little and muttering darkly to itself about the vicissitudes of an ocean voyage. Bad enough it had ruined the only container it had been able to drag halfway across the world; bad enough it would probably catch its metaphorical, not to mention metaphysical, death because its elegant attire was soggy like unto a sponge; and bad enough its stomach was growling since it couldn't even remember the last time it had eaten a decent meal.

It sneezed.

Its mouth felt funny.

And definitely bad enough that when its container had hit that damn boulder, it had awakened with such a start, and so ready to feed, that its head had burst through the wood and smacked into the rock.

It hoped it could do with one tooth for a while; it hoped that regeneration included a dental plan.

Yes, all that was bad enough.

But what was worse was the storm.

It hated storms.

The shadow wished, just once, it could make an entrance without a lot of bother. Just walk into town, greet the citizens, smile at the children, set up housekeeping in a conveniently deserted mansion, and get to work. No fuss, no mess, and a full set of dry for a change clothes. And no one understanding until it was too late why it had arrived.

Storms, on the other hand, were warnings.

Wherever the shadow went there was always some idiot out there who knew that bad things happened whenever there was an unexpected storm of somewhat biblical proportions. Which sooner or later alerted the populace and made house-hunting a bitch, not to mention the feeding.

Just once.

That's all it asked.

A spring evening with a full moon, stars, a gentle breeze, things like that.

It sneezed.

It reached the main street and glared at the empty sidewalks, the dark windows.

That was the other thing.

Every time there was a storm people stayed inside, and how the hell was it supposed to do what it was supposed to do when there was no one around to do it to?

Sonofabitch.

A sigh, then, that ripped an awning off a pawn shop, and made a bolt of lightning head for New Hampshire.

It was hungry.

It was pissed.

It was wet.

Any thought of waiting another day to grab a bite vanished in a spurt of not inconsiderable temper.

Out there . . . somewhere out there . . . was breakfast, damn-it. There always was. Some full-fledged beanhead who didn't know enough to come in out of the rain. Always. It never failed.

The shadow stretched a little, shook the rain from its cloak, and *changed*.

And, as it sprinted across the street, it *howled* . . .
and sneezed.

Somewhere in Assyria, in Maine, in the dark, a nervous dog began to bay at the unseen moon.

Purity Horton, on the other hand, wasn't nervous at all; she was, in fact, mad enough to chew nails and spit rust.

First there was that fatheaded but sinewy-thighed Buddy

Plimsol, who had taken her out for dinner, drinks, and a few clumsy turns on the dance floor at the MooseRack Dining Salon and Bar, after which he had driven her halfway up Nachey Mountain to the delightful seclusion of Lovers Ledge. Once there, and while a hell of a storm slashed and raged around his windshield-steamed automobile, it became swiftly apparent that he expected willing, nay even eager, compensation for his charming company and witty Down East repartee. He even attempted to twirl his pencil-line mustache.

Now, while Purity was not ordinarily averse to a little slap-and-tickle, giggle-and-grunt, and some acrobatic high kicking in the name of love and neighborly relations, she was always repelled by heavy-handed masculine attitudes of right-of-passage, especially when she was the one expected to pay the tolls. When he persisted and she demurred, when he begged and she refused, when he finally demanded and she blew her stack, he commanded that she give him something to remember her by since she could be damn sure this was the last time he was going to waste his hard-earned money on a woman with a name like that. What he received was an expertly severe boxing of the ears and a deft set of knuckles to his limited personal fortune, after which she received in turn a boot out the door and the smell of his exhaust.

Then there was the mountain itself. Heavily wooded with pine and fir, oak and maple, its not terribly steep eastern slope was broken only by the aforementioned prow-shaped outcropping and a paved, narrow, switchback road that made riding to the summit a torturous affair because of its serpentine twists and unnatural bends, most of which had signs cautioning downward-bound drivers not to go too fast or they'd probably end up in Heaven's Path cemetery before first light.

Lastly, there was the storm.

Purity didn't mind the boot from the car, not all that much, because now Buddy would be so thoroughly embroiled in contemporary male guilt that she'd probably be able to castrate him without lifting a finger, and get some nice new jewelry, and another meal, in the bargain; nor did she mind the road, because there were connecting trails between each straightaway which, in daylight, tended to cut several hours off a homeward trip if

you didn't mind a few snags and deadfalls and the occasional
curious moose.

She did, however, mind the storm.

After exhausting its initial fury, it had calmed itself slightly,
even as she trudged through blowing leaves and twigs, lightning spitting at the distant water, thunder echoing through the
flanking hills, the distinct scent of additional rain making her
shiver and pull her pearl-studded cardigan closer about her
shoulders. She hated the rain. It messed her hair, made the
streets smell funny, and this time of year raised a mist from the
ground that looked all too much like bewildered ghosts looking
for a way to get back to their graves.

The wind blew harder.

The trees, now and again leaping into view on the heels of
flaring lightning, were too dark, too close together, too tall and
dark for comfort.

Thunder rolled off the ocean on the backs of huge breakers.
Making her jump, making her angry because she had jumped,
making her break into a cautious, angry trot fueled by the idea
that as soon as she reached bottom, she would go straight back
to the Dining Salon and take Buddy's nose off with the ice tongs
her father kept behind the bar.

But the anger lasted only until she heard the wolf.

At first she didn't believe it. A stray dog from town maybe,
pretending to be a wolf, but certainly not the real thing. There
were never wolves in the forest. Hadn't been for ages. In fact,
the last wolf she had ever heard of had last been seen thirty
years ago, and that had turned out to be an abandoned German
shepherd which had, upon closer investigation, turned out to
be nothing more than an extremely hairy Berlin tourist with no
English and a lousy sense of humor.

A wolf?

It is, she thought, to laugh.

Lightning.

She looked back.

Laughter was the last thing that sprang to mind.

Berlin, however, sounded pretty damn good.

She yelped involuntarily.

A reasonably large, fanged, yellow-eyed lupine creature

stood solemnly in the middle of the road, and though she was but a simple barkeep's daughter, she knew damn well the difference between a collie and what she saw.

Lightning.

The wolf was gone, into the forest.

The trot became a slow canter.

Had she imagined it?

In the lulls between the cannonade of thunder and the fusillade of lightning, she was dismayed to hear the slavering beast tracking her relentlessly, just out of sight in the trees.

All right, she thought, it's not your imagination, so what are you going to do about it?

What she did, when the animal growled menacingly, was curse Buddy Plimsol, his car, and his hands, and run full-out, sweeping around each bend, sprinting along the straightaways, gasping for air, suddenly drenched and frozen when the next stroke of lightning reopened the clouds.

The wolf followed.

She saw its eyes, yellow and slanted, whenever she dared a glance to either side.

She heard its muttering grunts and sharp, terrifying barks whenever she slowed down to catch her breath.

She knew she shouldn't be afraid. All the experts said wolves only attacked the weak and the helpless, the sick and the lame. And they only attacked when they were hungry.

It howled hungrily.

Purity decided the experts were jerks, and probably dead.

There was only one thing to do now, one way to elude it, and she took it without hesitation: abruptly she veered off the road and plunged down a footworn trail barely wide enough to contain her, slapping branches aside, leaping fallen logs, breaking into the open and plunging into the trees again on the other side. A branch snagged her sweater and she yelled as she slapped at it frantically, realized what had happened, and shrugged out of the cardigan and cast it aside; another branch tangled her hair momentarily, and she shrieked; an invisible rock tripped her, and she slid a full yard before regaining her feet.

This wasn't an adventure anymore.

There was a wolf.

There was the storm.

And there, just below, the first lights of Assyria as the slope leveled and the trees began to thin.

In the open again, she skidded to a halt.

"Oh," she said.

It stood on the opposite shoulder, grey and black and as high as her waist, slavering fangs bared in an evil semblance of a smile.

Frantically she searched the road, the ground, for something to use as a weapon.

Directly behind her she found a stout branch and grabbed for it and turned in a crouch that told the beast it wasn't going to get her without a fight, ask Buddy if it didn't believe her.

It was gone.

Lightning.

Her mouth opened in stark terror.

Thunder.

In its place was something else.

The high, mournful keening of a storm-born wind.

And Purity Horton screamed bloody murder.

- II -

Three Weeks
Of
Bad Stuff

·1·

Time passed.
  The dog howled a lot.
  Hoarsely.

·2·

Dwight Lepeche was a scruffy little man whose razor never quite managed to catch all the whiskers on his florid, pudgy face. His colorless hair was stringy, his eyes beady, his lips generally aquiver with either indignation or anticipation. His mother had once told him, in a rare moment of levity, that while she was carrying him she'd been frightened either by a weasel or an Edsel, she never could remember which. Not that it mattered. He knew he wasn't handsome, knew that people shied away from his approach, and knew that things, and his appearance, could be worse. He could, after all, look like his mother. Rest her soul.

But at the moment, none of that mattered.

What mattered was surviving long enough to reach his destination without catching double pneumonia or falling down a ravine and breaking his leg.

Dwight did not like the woods.

Nor, when he thought about it, did he think it at all contradictory that, as a hunter by trade and a poacher by avocation, he did not like the woods. Any sane man would hate the woods. They were too natural. They didn't do what you told them, didn't listen when you yelled at them, didn't expend a single dollop of mercy when you were hurt in them, and probably deliberately rearranged themselves when you were half the time lost and couldn't see the nose in front of your face.

Which was why he was puzzled.

Right now, he should be back home, sitting cozily in his three-room plywood shack on the other side of Nachey Mountain, working on the fifth volume of his memoirs and the fifth of scotch hidden under the couch for emergencies; instead, he was slogging through the middle of a forest heading for someplace he went to only when he was in need of supplies, a couple of drinks at a bar instead of his kitchen table, or a few moments alone with the woman of his dreams, assuming she wasn't tied up with a previous customer, although he had never been into that rope-and-feather stuff himself.

He hadn't planned on going into town for at least another month.

But here he was, stomping through the woods anyway, and he wasn't even horny.

In many vital ways, then, he was terrified.

He just didn't do things like this.

Yet, strangely enough, he was also excited, and unnervingly close to elated.

Because of the Voice.

Normally, unless he was drunk out of his mind and looking for something to cut up or beat up or skin and wear home, he was respectful of the dangerous face of Nature's mysterious night. In such circumstance, such as after the sun went down, he usually stayed home. He slept. He ate. He drank. He listened to the radio. He worked on his life story, which was now up to the summer of '42, just a few months shy of the event of his birth. Tonight, however, protected by a frayed hunting jacket, a hunting cap with its flaps loose and flapping, and calf-high boots, he was heading toward town and, in between flashes of pure sanity, not really minding.

Because of the Voice.

It had come to him just as the moon had risen over the western mountains. A soft voice. An insistent voice. A caring voice. A voice whose loving inflections and daring insinuations reminded him of his paternal grandfather, rest his soul. A voice that told him that, for the first time in his miserable, petty, disgusting little poaching life, he was needed.

For what, he did not know.

For whom, he did not care.

All he knew was that the Voice urged him to come hither without delay.

And he came.

Weaponless.

Defenseless.

Every so often having a truly foul but not necessarily vile urge to munch on a spider.

At such moments the Voice chuckled understandingly and assured him that the craving was quite all right, spiders were nutritional and too damn ugly to live anyway; but each time he came upon a sheltered web and saw its maker trembling against the elements, he couldn't bring himself to do it. All those legs, that fat little body, those horrid beady eyes . . . it was too much like shaving.

Ants, he decided after a spate of hard thinking; he'd start with ants and work his way up.

That's all right, too, the Voice responded gently; ants are okay, but stay away from those cockroaches, you don't know where they've been.

Dwight listened to the Voice.

He did not know why, nor did he question its origin.

He only knew that, come hell or high water, he had to obey.

The Voice chuckled its approval.

Time passed.

Dwight paused at the edge of a small clearing to get his bearings. It was difficult, in the dark, trying to figure out where he was in the woods even though he had lived here all his life, but a glimpse of a familiar mountain silhouette gave him all the information he needed. In only two or three hours, all things being equal and the creek don't rise, he would be at the summit; a couple of hours later, midnight at the latest, unless he fell and took the quick way, he'd be in town.

He would be in Assyria, in Maine.

Waiting for the Voice to give him guidance, comfort, and the first truly honorable goal he'd ever had in his life.

He grinned.

A wolf howled in the distance.

He laughed.

And the wind began to rise.

Jared Graverly rose as well, though perhaps with a bit more lusty enthusiasm—yelling and screaming at the top of his gravelly voice and bouncing around on his four-poster platform bed and throwing king-size pillows against the far wall and kicking off the blankets and yelling and screaming some more.

When he finished, his face aglow with perspiration and his lungs straining for air, he gasped, "Lord."

The woman reclining seductively beside him smacked his arm. "Watch your mouth, Jared."

Instantly abashed, fearfully humbled, he covered his eyes with one hand, resisting the temptation to peek through his fingers as she slipped away from him. "Sorry. Lost my head for a moment. It won't happen again."

A rustle of royal blue satin sheets.

A soft padding across the thick red carpet.

The sound of the bedroom door opening softly.

Graverly swallowed dryly and wiped a corner of the sheet over his face. "Must you leave already?"

"Alas."

He knelt on the mattress, a handmade Amish comforter tucked coyly around his legs. "But it seems like you just got here," he complained.

"I know," said the sleek shadow standing sexily in the doorway. "But I cannot stay. You know I cannot stay. You know I must leave. You know I must go. You know all this, and still you insist?"

He nodded.

She sighed.

He held out a hand, beseeching her mutely.

Outside, several houses away, a dog howled mournfully.

"Damn that thing," he snarled. "Why the hell doesn't Mabel shut it up?"

The suggestive hush of expensive imported rustling silk as the shadow stepped over the threshold and paused. "You are too impatient, my love," the shadow whispered, a shadow-hand blowing him a kiss. "You must learn to appreciate that which comes with the night."

He knew that. He knew he knew that. But knowing it didn't make either her leaving or that damned dog's baying any easier to take. Nevertheless, he also knew that she knew that he knew that any untoward pressure on his part would ruin everything. She would leave him. He knew that. She would never speak to him again, nor would she grace his bed with her animalistic presence, nor would she continue to deposit great sums of cash into his private Swiss bank account.

He knew that.

She knew he knew it because she laughed softly, deep in her swanlike throat, and he shivered uncomfortably because, for a moment there, her laugh sounded altogether too much like a large dog growling. Not Mabel Horton's dog; that thing was a Scottie with pretensions to Godzillahood. He meant a really large dog, with really large teeth and really large claws and a really huge appetite.

With an effort that made his greasy hair sway over his smooth but streaked brow, he composed himself, slid a hand through his locks, and cleared his throat. "I imagine I'll get to meet . . . him . . . soon?"

The shadow nodded.

"People talk, you know."

"Yes."

"I mean, it's hard sometimes, because they've never seen him, you know what I mean?"

"I do."

He forced a laugh. "A couple of people, they don't even think he exists. How ridiculous."

She remained silent.

A slight chill walked across his bare shoulders. "Look," he said urgently, more urgently than he wanted. "I want you . . . I'd like you to tell him that I've done everything he's asked, all right? I mean, people talk and spread rumors, you know how small towns are, but I've managed to head most of them off at the pass, as it were. It's important that he understand that he has nothing to worry about."

"Oh," she answered, "fear not. He knows."

Relieved but fighting to keep that relief from showing since it wouldn't do to exhibit any weakness at this critical juncture, he nodded and asked when they would be able to meet again.

The door began to close. "Soon," she promised sincerely. "Very soon."

He nodded gratefully.

"But only after," she added sternly, "you have taken care of that last little tiny business matter or three or four. They are too essential to our . . . future. But then . . . oh then, my darling, will you know what it is like to—"

The door closed.

Graverly waited for several minutes before assuring himself that he was at last alone, waited several minutes more to be sure that he was really sure, then hugged himself in excitement and delicious apprehension. He shifted to sit on the edge of the mattress and stared out the window and over Beachfront Avenue to the beach beyond. There were no buildings on the other side of the road. It was a law. It was, in fact, a law he had helped pass since he didn't want to look out of his downstairs office window into a bait shop all day. Not that he was against fishing, he went to lunch with fishermen all the time, but there was something about a Christmas display of worms and fish heads that tended to make him nauseous, or nervous, depending on what sort of deal he was involved in.

He didn't care now.

Soon he would be the man who owned the whole damn place.

Not politically, not emotionally, not financially, not spiritually.

Physically.

Own it.

Every last grain of sand, every weed, every garage, every tire swing in a tree, every fruit cellar, every shack . . . everything.

His.

All his.

He sneezed.

The wind rose and taunted his bedroom window, knocking on the pane and running away.

He sneezed again and drew the comforter closely around his shoulders, straightened without standing, and wondered if he'd be able to catch a glimpse of *her* as she made her way home to wherever it was she lived. He never had before; he probably wouldn't be able to now, but it didn't stop him from trying. From the bed, that is. If he stood at the window, she would see him. He knew that. And if she saw him, if she knew he was disobeying her explicit orders never to attempt to locate her or the place where she lived, she would probably bite his teeth out by the roots. Except for the caps. Those she'd probably hammer out with a chisel.

He didn't want that.

He liked his teeth, and he was mad about her, and to get her, all he had to do was conclude those few simple transactions, get those few final contracts signed, get those last few damned names on the dotted lines, and all he could see—or would be able to see if he were standing up and looking out the window— would be all his.

Then, with one stroke of a fountain pen he'd bought in Boston last year, he would sell it to her.

And to *him*.

And be rich.

Not just ordinary rich or even filthy rich.

He'd be so goddamned stinking rich he would be able to take that goddamned poor excuse for a dog of Mabel Horton's, rip its heart out, stuff what was left, mount it on the hood of his car, and drive at top speed all the way to his new estate in the Everglades without so much as a single stupid cop pulling him over because they'd know who he was because of the dog mounted on the hood.

He giggled.

He laughed.

He rolled onto his back and kicked his legs gleefully in the air.

And if those goddamned idiots wouldn't sell their property, then he would personally and with great satisfaction murder them all. Especially Kent Montana. In broad daylight. Then buy the damned places at public auction. Especially Kent Montana's.

Either way, one way or another, that pompous son of a bitch was doomed.

The dog howled.

Jared Graverly howled back.

"It's like I told you," said Lavinia Volle, wiry hair wrapped in a kerchief, her cardigan buttoned as close to her neck as her aging bosom would allow. "The man comes around offering me a zillion dollars for this old place—the place where I was born, mind you—I tell him to shove it up his grease gun, and he tells me there ain't nothing in the world gonna stop him from taking my very own house away from me."

"I don't believe it," Frieda Juleworth answered.

"Why not? I just told you, didn't I?"

"I know you did. I just don't believe it."

"You saying I'm a liar, Frieda?"

"How can you say that?"

"In English, German, a little Portuguese if pressed, and pig Latin."

In a huff, Frieda adjusted the bulky sweater she wore on account of the chill in the air, then plucked at some lint clinging to her black corduroy trousers. "I ain't calling you a liar, Lavinia."

Lavinia considered for a few minutes before deciding to be magnanimous and accept the apology.

"I just don't see how this place is worth a zillion dollars. I mean, it's lovely enough, don't get me wrong, dear, but he only offered me a half a mil for mine. And it ain't half as big as yours, if you don't count the swimming pool with the cabana and all."

Lavinia slammed a fist against her heart. "I'll be."

Frieda nodded sharply. "Showed me the check right there in his alligator skin briefcase. I told him what he could do with the briefcase, and he told me to go jump in a grave." She snorted derisively. "Like I would, you know? I dig 'em, I don't use 'em. Yep. Bold as brass without the balls, that's what I calls him. Fat lot he knows about graves, anyway."

The Assyrian gravediggers rocked a little, hummed a little, listened to a damn dog howling on the other side of town.

The wind toyed with the hanging ivy dangling from Grecian urns nailed to the railing.

"Y'know," Lavinia said, keeping her voice low as if imparting a secret she'd been sworn to keep, "he told *me* he was acting on behalf of someone called the Count."

Frieda nodded in sage agreement. "Me, too. Count Something or other."

"Think he's related to the baron?"

"By marriage, maybe. Foreigners are always marrying their cousins and such." Frieda cackled. "Like old Dwight. Way I heard it, his mother had, you know, relations, with the back end of an Edsel."

Lavinia scoffed. "You mean *in* the back end of an Edsel."

"Ain't the way I heard it."

An owl hooted.

The pines whispered urgently to themselves as the wind grew stronger.

Down on Beachfront, a car backfired.

Twice.

"I tell you, Frieda, there is something damn mysterious going on around here," Lavinia said at last. "That greasy little twerp ain't had two whole dimes to rub together since he sold that old bathhouse to Reverend Ardlaw for the Thursday night baptisms and such." A grime-encrusted hand scratched the hooked tip of her hawk nose thoughtfully. "Something mighty mysterious, if you ask me."

"Well, I ain't getting baptized, that's for damn sure."

"Damnit, Frieda, you already are."

"Yeah, but that was a long time ago. I think you gotta renew it now and again, make sure it sticks."

The dog howled.

It was answered by a wolf.

"That was a wolf," Frieda said, leaning forward to look up the street.

"No wolves."

"Damn big dog, then."

They both looked up the street, but all they could see were the tall iron gates to Heaven's Path, and no wolf in his right mind would set paw in the cemetery. Not after dark. Besides which, there weren't no wolves around here and hadn't been for decades, so it must have been a big dog that wouldn't set paw in Heaven's Gate.

Lavinia shuddered.

Frieda shivered.

And when a fairly large black thing flew past them at not much higher than eye level, Lavinia eased herself out of the chair and said, "Think I'm gonna take a bath."

Frieda gaped. "Tonight?"

"Why? There a law against baths on Friday nights?"

Frieda peered into the dark, trying to bring to a picture the thing she had seen. "Need someone to wash your hair?"

"No," said Lavinia, "but you could hold the gun."

- III -

The
Good Guys

◆ **1** ◆

The sea, so vast and uncompromising in its seductive beauty, is nevertheless no place for cowards. Battleships sink in it, ocean liners vanish on it, hurricanes are spawned over it, and sharks swim malevolently below its surface. It devours entire islands and modifies continents, grinds rock to sand and spits volcanos at the sky; though it provides food for thought, its lethal poisons are innumerable; and while whales sing and dolphins glide and flying fish leap and starfish feed dreams, there's also a whole lot of pretty damn ugly stuff swimming around down there.

And icebergs, thought Kent Montana; let's not forget the bloody icebergs. Sneaky buggers for their size. Always creeping about in their own private fog banks. Sinking unsinkable ships and the like. All in all, a thoroughly nasty piece of natural business.

But one he wouldn't mind seeing about now. It would, unquestionably, lend a little cachet of excitement to a rather dull visit.

On the other hand, dull is what he had originally hoped for when he decided to come.

When he had received the message.

He grunted softly.

The message.

• • •

Lordship.
Help, we need somebody.
Help!
Not just anybody . . . you!
Please!
What I mean to say is, I don't know if you're planning on com-
ing up this way anytime soon what with all your movies and all
keeping you so busy you don't hardly have time to visit anymore,
but it would sure help if you would. Visit, that is. We got a prob-
lem. A serious problem. You're the only man who can help. If
you don't come, we'll all die. You're all we have left, except for a
little fat guy with a beard, and he ain't worth piss on a salt lick.
Sure could use you
Help.
Meet you at the wall.
Your friend.

The message was unsigned.

Originally he had thought it a decidedly unfunny prank, or one
of Roxanne Lott's frequent excursions into fantasy; originally,
after nearly getting killed during an interview in Louisiana for
a film that, as it turned out, didn't exist, he had planned to fly
back to his baronial estate on an unnamed Hebrides isle and hang
out for a while, wench a little with the village twins, check the
winery and the cattle, bribe his mother's assassins to leave him
alone, then put out a contract on his agent.

But the more he had thought about it, the more uneasy he had
felt.

Strange messages didn't come along every day.

Of course, there was some unpleasant stuff in there about
dying, which didn't exactly get his heroic juices flowing. On
the other hand, he had spent several wonderfully lazy summers
in Assyria, in Maine, during the hiatus of his daytime drama,
Passions and Power, of which he was no longer a part thanks
to a thankless director. The town had become his refuge, his
temporary home away from home.

Now something seemed to be threatening it.

So he'd come.

So here he was.

And there wasn't, thankfully, a whole lot of shaking going on around here.

It was, as always, dull.

Just the way he usually liked it.

Unfortunately, no one he'd spoken to thus far seemed to know who had sent him the mysterious note, and dull, by now, was getting pretty damn boring.

He took a deep breath. He slipped his hands into his denim jacket pockets. He watched without much interest the masts of the fishing fleet bob on the horizon, heading toward their marina at the north end of town, below the rocky headland. Not many vessels, but diligent and hard-working, and sufficiently selective in their catches to insure that Assyrian cod and haddock commanded the interest and the dollars of piscine connoisseurs from Connecticut to Florida. Personally he couldn't stand the stuff— or anything with fins, for that matter—especially when it was displayed on beds of shaved ice in the market, glassy eyes glaring reproachfully at you, scales gleaming, mouths gaping accusingly; thank you very much, he thought, but I prefer a good steak any day.

Nevertheless, since there weren't any icebergs, it was something to look at.

The town he knew by heart.

It stretched along two miles of rugged Maine coastline, bounded on the east by the Atlantic Ocean, and on the west by the not terribly tall, pine-choked slopes of Nachey Mountain. Its harbor was formed by a low, bare-rock arm to the south used mainly by landloving fishermen of the more sedate variety, and a headland to the north of jumbled rocks and imposing cliffs atop which sat an empty stone mansion purportedly constructed in the late eighteenth century. Oddly enough, the mansion had no name.

Aside from the fishing, there were several cottage industries as well, including sweater-weaving, moose-antler fabrication, and taxidermy for those marine and forest creatures not commercial or palatable enough to be sold as is but big or cute or ferocious enough to be mounted on a plank, varnished, and sold as big game trophies. There were also a handful of small restaurants for those travelers passing through, a couple of bars, two small hotels, and the usual run of local commerce.

Its most prominent feature, however, was its centuries-old sea wall.

There were no buildings on the oceanward side of the main street; instead, there was a thirty-foot wide, well-kept pedestrian park of grass-and-pebble that served as a buffer between Beachfront Avenue and a flat-topped, waist-high wall made of hardy Maine stone. Every fifty yards or so there was a gap with stone stairs that led down to the beach, seven feet below the level of the land.

The wall itself stretched for over a mile.

No one knew who had built it, and the only time anyone cared was when a piece of it fell down on a tourist sunning himself on the sand. Lawsuits, however, were infrequent; the wall was damn heavy.

The townspeople themselves minded their own business and expected others to do the same. They knew, for example, that Kent was a Scots baron, knew that he was an actor, and knew what his mother looked like in case she tried a night assault over the Nachey summit. They didn't care. He paid his taxes, paid his bills, and seldom asked stupid questions. Thus, he was accepted. Not as one of them; he talked too funny for that. But as a semi-resident with squatting rights.

A black-masked sea gull banked low over the water, dipped, and returned to the air with something dark and wriggling in its beak.

He sniffed.

He took his hands out of his pockets and snapped his fingers, looked around, sniffed, looked back at the water and sniffed again.

The sun had already slipped below the top of the mountain, luring tentative shadows out of the sidestreets and a desultory breeze out of the trees.

A buoy clanged its melancholy tune out on the water.

Eventually, the streetlamps flared on.

The breeze took on a chill, and he flipped up his collar.

If whoever sent the message didn't meet him soon, he was going to go home, the hell with it.

But if the message was accurate, not a sick practical joke, then something had to be done.

He turned and leaned against the wall, folded his arms across his chest and tucked in his chin.

That wasn't it.

A distant tingling in his stomach suggested that perhaps he ought to stop sitting on the wall and go get something to eat. By his watch it was just gone seven and, since he hadn't the energy to walk the mile and a half back to his solitary cottage on the beach, it might be a wise thing to pay a visit to the MooseRack Dining Salon and Bar, or the Lobster Is Inn, and stoke the fires for that return journey. A hearty meal, a drink or two, and he'd be ready for anything. Even bored.

The sound of someone walking slowly down the pebbled path from his left.

He looked.

A heavily muscled figure hobbled toward him wearing a sea captain's cap, short-sleeved striped shirt, and an ivory-and-teak pegleg carved in the shape of a bird's evil claw, whence the man got his colorful name.

"Evening, sir," the figure called in its usual hoarse voice, the kind that made Kent want to clear his throat every thirty seconds.

"Evening, Claw."

"Lovely night, ain't it."

"Aye, it is that."

Closer, and he was able to see the full black beard, the heavy black eyebrows, the thrice-broken nose, and the deep-set eyes that lent the man a certain air of piracy the vulture perched on his left shoulder somehow failed to convey. Claw Tackard walked the streets all day, all night, doing odd jobs, passing gossip from one household to another, entertaining the tourists with his tales of stirring adventure on the high seas while collecting their donations, and playing his finger-worn concertina. He wasn't the town character so much as he was, in essence, Assyria itself—pleasant, hard-working, and just a little nuts.

Claw hoisted himself easily onto the wall, wriggled his pegleg around a little, settled the vulture, brushed a pebble to the ground, then took off his cap and scratched through his frizzy white hair.

"You just dock in these parts?"

Kent nodded. "Came in just after midnight. Drove up from New York."

"Argh, aye," the pirate said, and lifted what was left of his right leg so he could knock the sand from his claw. Then he adjusted the concertina slung over his shoulder. Then he took a loud deep breath.

"You didn't, by chance, send me a message, did you, Claw?"

The pirate shook his head, adjusted his black captain's cap, spat away from the prevailing wind, and belched.

Kent made no comment, but he sensed that something was bothering the Assyrian pirate. Ordinarily, Claw was not the apprehensive or pensive type. He laughed Death in the face. He lived for adventure. He had conned and had been conned by the best in the world and never a word of complaint passed his lips.

But tonight . . .

Kent glanced at the full moon rising over Nachey Mountain, shivered a little when the breeze tickled the back of his neck. Ghosts of thin clouds slipped over the stars. He nodded up the street toward a flickering neon antler. "I've been thinking about dinner."

"Food is good," Claw allowed thoughtfully. "You don't eat, you die. Argh, sir, many's the time I almost died on remote desert islands for lack of a decent meal to fill me poor empty belly." He laughed nostalgically, chucked the vulture good-naturedly under its beak, patted its wrinkled red head, and whistled tunelessly through the gap in his teeth. "Lots of times, as a matter of fact."

Time passed.

The traffic passed.

The moon rose higher.

An eighteen-wheeler blasted through town, kicking up scraps of paper from the gutters, leaving nothing behind but a swirling cloud of dust.

"I could use some company," Kent said.

The pirate laughed again, ruefully, and slapped his knee. "Sir, you don't want an old sea dog like me to share your table.

Nosir. You want a gorgeous woman with a figure like the sea in full wave and a voice like the wind that ruffles your sails on a warm summer's evening such as we have tonight." He gestured grandly. "You want a woman who will run barefoot through your hair, scrub your back with a giant natural sponge from the sultry waters off Greece, bring you a crystal glass brimming with champagne and feed you fat juicy grapes while you lie on the beach and watch the tide reach hungrily for her wanton beauty." He nodded wisely and adjusted his cap. "Aye, sir, you don't want the like of me to dine with you this night."

Damn, Kent thought; he's right.

"Still, I wouldn't say no."

Damn.

The buoy rang mournfully.

"But I think," the pirate continued reluctantly, "this old buccaneer is going to make it an early night this evening, your lordship. No offense."

"No, of course not," Kent replied. "But this isn't like you, you know. A free meal. Free drinks. I don't mean to pry, but . . . is something wrong?"

"No," the man insisted, too quickly.

Kent looked at him.

"Just feeling a bit of the old ache in my old pirate bones, is all."

Kent looked at him.

"Old Bruno's feeling a little peckish, too."

Kent looked at him.

Claw finally looked back.

Kent gave him an encouraging nod.

Claw stroked the vulture's neck absently as he licked his lips and checked the length of the street for potential interruption. "It's the night, matey sir, you see," he admitted at last, rasping voice low, and just shy of a quiver. "Been walking these mean streets for nearly thirty years since my last ship went down in a fiery blaze off the Madagascar coast, been hunting and fishing and a few things I can't mention for longer than you've been alive. I know this place like the back of me old hands." He inhaled slowly, deeply.

"And there's something wrong out there tonight. A terrible thing about to happen. Argh, aye, a . . . terrible thing."

The pirate, Kent thought, had either taken one too many bottles of yo-ho rum, or he'd been scratching himself too hard with his foot. Nevertheless, and thoroughly against his better judgment, bored or not:

"What?" he asked quietly.

"Don't know."

"A feeling?"

After a long moment, the pirate swallowed hard and nodded.

Kent glanced over his shoulder at the deserted beach, at the flashing white of the foam in the moonlight. He knew about feelings. They happened to him all the time and usually just before he was about to confront the method of his unplanned demise.

The problem was, trouble wasn't exactly the way he had hoped his boredom would end.

Then he puffed his cheeks, thrust the feeling about the feeling aside, and asked himself if he could believe, seriously believe, mind you, the mutterings of a nutter who thought himself the reincarnation of Long John Silver. A good man he was, and a hell of a storyteller. Loyal. Fierce in his devotion to his friends. But he didn't always have all his sails turned to the wind.

"Bruno agrees with me, sir. Been off his feed all day."

Bruno, Kent thought, is a vulture.

And not for the first time was he tempted to inquire about the curious bird, and not for the first time did he stifle that same temptation. It was not for him to ask why the pirate didn't have a gaudy parrot that sang salty songs and talked dirty to the ladies, and it was not for him to know why the pirate had named his laconic companion Bruno, and it definitely was not for him to query the nature of whatever horrid avian disease it was that had rendered that fearsome creature completely without its natural covering.

Not that the bird cared.

It was dead.

It just looked godawful, that's all, all those feathers missing and its beak kind of just hanging there half open. You looked at it long enough, you expected it to start drooling. You also thought it might be a rubber chicken.

An idea occurred to him then, and he rubbed a thumb under his nose, cleared his throat. Changed his mind. It wasn't possible. On the other hand, Claw knew things most men weren't meant to know, and when they knew them regretted it. He cleared his throat again. "We're . . . we're not talking about my mother here, are we, Claw?"

The pirate laughed quickly and without mirth. "Argh, sir, we're talking about something far worse than her, believe me. Argh."

"You don't know my mother. How can you be sure—"

He never finished.

Suddenly, something huge and black streaked out of the gathering dark above them, slammed into his head and knocked him off the wall.

Backward.

The last thing he heard before he hit the sand, and a rather dramatically placed rock, was Claw Tackard, bellowing bloody murder.

Professor Sloan Tarkingdale did not like dogs, wrinkled handkerchiefs, or people who wore belts that didn't match their shoes. He didn't like airplanes, either. They were too big, they were too crowded, and they tended to fall down when they were supposed to fly up. And stay there. He much preferred his expensively shod feet, his British racing green Jaguar, and express trains, in that order, to get him from one dangerous, life-threatening assignment to another. He left the ground only when he had to, and only, preferably, under severe sedation and after a long visit to the airport chapel. But Time, this time, was not on his side, no it wasn't, and taking a luxury liner from his home base in London's West End would have consumed too many precious hours. Too many people were in danger. Too many lives would be lost. Too many souls slipped away. Too many opportunities missed. As it was, he feared that he was already too late for the beginning. And having missed the beginning, the end was too disastrous, too chilling, too thoroughly nasty to contemplate.

So, courage firmly in his sweaty grip, which had wrinkled his suits to no end, he had flown from London to Boston's Logan Airport.

He had driven up the coast to Assyria, in Maine.

He had taken the best room available at the SurfSide Hotel, and now he stood on the small semicircular balcony, purple silk dressing gown with black velvet lapels in place, goatee neatly trimmed, curved pipe smoking, as he watched the night creep over this place, turning the sea black, the beach grey, and his mood sour.

Several days had passed since his arrival, and nothing had happened.

He had even taken it upon himself to attempt an examination of the turret-corner stone mansion that had no name over there on the headland. It was the perfect spot for what he sought, almost a necessity for his enemy, but the only road leading to it had been blocked by fallen trees, boulders, and uprooted shrubbery. He later discovered that there was in fact another way—by boat, to a small, boiling-sea cove at the headland's Atlantic face, where, he had been told, he could find stairs carved into the rock. Lots of them. He decided the examination would have to wait until his jet-lag had left him.

It was discouraging.

All the signs and portents, all his years of training, all his professorially honed skills of deduction and ratiocination had pointed to this very spot for the next great battle, perhaps the greatest of his career.

And nothing had happened.

He brought the pipe to his lips and puffed in agitation, and a hint of despair.

Pedestrians casually walked the street below; automobiles passed slowly, their unseen occupants once in a while calling a friendly greeting to those on the sidewalk; up at the marina, the lonely sound of ships' bells; from various nightspots along Beachfront Avenue, the muffled joy of music and people laughing.

Lord, he thought, didn't they know?

Didn't they understand?

"Sloan, stop posing."

Slowly he turned his carefully maintained leonine head toward the balcony immediately to his left, the one that belonged to the connecting room. He stared at the woman standing there.

Didn't she know?

Didn't she understand?

Obviously not, when he noted the disdainful but patient look she gave him. She was, even for the longtime personal assistant of an incredibly wealthy man whose entire adult life had been dedicated to the eradication of Evil wherever and whenever it was unearthed, breathtakingly beautiful. Flowing black hair that nestled softly upon her shoulders, deep and intelligent black eyes, full red lips, a figure that made palms sweaty and fingers twitch, a—

"Sloan, knock it off."

"What? What?"

She shook her head lovingly. "First you act as if these balconies are going to collapse and we're going to drop out of the sky like a stone any minute now even if we are only on the second floor. Then you act as if you want to tear off all my clothes and ravish me right here in the semi-dark where no one would know except maybe those two men in the park across the street. And I think one of them is a pirate."

He blinked.

She smiled.

He cleared his throat. Puffed his pipe. "You are wrong, Dianna. I am simply deeply concerned that we will not achieve our goal in time."

Her nod was thoughtful as she turned to the sea, to the eternal rolling black where no doubt a tidal wave was preparing to smash Assyria flat. He didn't much like the sea, either. It had too much water.

"Yes," she said, "I can see that."

He lowered his voice and leaned closer, only the railing, several potted plants, and the generous expanse of his girth preventing him from climbing over and seeking comfort in her arms, a prospect which, while it made him temporarily giddy, was also out of the question.

They were, after all, colleagues.

Business and pleasure do not mix.

And even if they did, he couldn't afford her.

"And if," he continued solemnly, "we don't find the fiend soon, who knows where he will put to ground? And if he does, how will we ever find him again? Have you seen all the trees around here? Thousands of them, for god's sake. And the mountains . . ." He rolled his eyes in distress. "How will I ever be to able to carry on the family hunting tradition if I fail and *he* remains free?" He sighed his dismay and placed a palm over his heart. "I don't want to disgrace my good name. And I don't want to plunge the world into chaos." He sighed again, closed his eyes, puffed his pipe. "I hate burdens, Dianna. No sooner do I shed one than another takes its place."

He felt her shift, and a cool finger reached through the foliage to touch his cheek.

"You're a good man, you know."

He shrugged. That much was obvious; it was the burdens part he hated.

"But this time you'll make it. This time will be the time that ends it all. Forever."

He hoped so. Lord, he dearly hoped so.

The balcony trembled when a breeze slipped down from the sharply peaked roof overhead.

He watched the two men down in the park holding, no doubt, some sort of mysterious sea-type conversation. Probably about fish.

"Can I have a raise?"

The one man, who didn't seem to be more than five-and-a-half feet tall to his expert eye, had something on his shoulder. He squinted, humphed. It was either a naked vulture or a rubber chicken.

"I said, can I have a raise?"

He chuckled benignly and blew a smoke ring. Dear, sweet, adorable, amusing Dianna Torne. Always there when he needed her, always ready with a clever quip or a quiet scold to put all things in perspective. Without question, she was a treasure, and an integral part of his never-ending crusade against the minions of the dark. Indeed, as he mused on, and pondered a little, how had he ever been able to destroy the craftily craven Creature of Cracow without her? What horrors would he have faced if she hadn't deciphered the clues that had led them to the successful annihilation of the infamous, albeit unknown to the public-at-large, Monster of Southwestern Munich? And all those others—

so many, many others!—who would have escaped his righteous wrath had it not been for her ready wit and perspicacity, her courage under fire, and her bravery under stress.

Of course, he had something to do with it too, or he wouldn't have become so respected and justifiably famous in certain esoteric circles.

It wasn't, he thought sullenly, as if she did *all* the work.

I mean, somebody around here has to read all those godawful musty tomes in languages no one in their right mind would want to speak in the first place except for a few bonkers monks. And somebody, for crying out loud, has to spend days deciphering the obscure diagrams and hellish arcane symbols and make sense of the omens and portents. And so what if she did all that too, it was his money that allowed her to do so, wasn't it? Why, if it hadn't been for him, for god's sake, she'd still be plying her trade in that ... that ... exorbitantly expensive *place* in Regent Street, that laughingly labeled Lonely Hearts Club, elegantly but expertly separating eager customers from their money in exchange for a few hours' pleasant company for dinner and dancing in a private club.

So what the hell was she after a raise for?

His well-tended eyebrows lowered a notch.

Was this a ploy, he wondered suspiciously. A trick? A ruse? Was it more than a raise she was after?

"Sloan, stop it."

Nuts.

The finger poked back through the potted plants and brushed across his manfully jutting chin with the beard on it and gave it a gentle flick.

"Just give me a raise."

A faint cry in the air, above and behind the hotel.

He frowned, cocked his head and listened. Was that the call of the demonic Devon Nighthawk, on the prowl for the souls of men who had just lost their wives in boating accidents?

He listened.

"All this travel and hunting and killing and stuff is all well and good, and don't think I don't appreciate your picking up the tabs along the way, because I do, but a girl has a private life, you know, and expenses. God, all those expenses! You wouldn't believe it even if I told you."

The cry came again.

No, not the Nighthawk.

Although it was just possible that it was the hunting siren of the supernaturally bent Owl of Jummara, seeking the pulsating livers of animals not previously protected by certain elaborate, and damn messy, rituals.

"I have bills."

Unless it was . . .

Unless it was . . .

Unless, at long last, it was . . .

Tarkingdale felt his stomach begin a slow crawl toward his throat.

"I mean, dressing in silk is nice once in a while, but it gets damn cold in winter, you know?"

The balcony quivered when the breeze gusted to a wind, and faded again.

"You ever try to wear silk underwear in Finland, in the middle of February?"

As a matter of fact, he thought—

"Besides," she whispered playfully, "if you don't give me a raise, I just may be too distracted to make a correct translation or interpretation the next time our lives depend upon it. I mean, not that I'd do it deliberately or anything, because you know how devoted I am to you, Sloan, but economic pressures and things . . . you know?"

The cry became a shriek.

Tarkingdale swallowed heavily.

One of the men across the way threw up a panicked hand, but not in time to prevent something huge, something black, from swooping out of the dark and knocking him ass-over-teakettle off the sea wall.

Tarkingdale gasped.

"So," said Dianna, "what do you think?"

The sand cooled rapidly once the sun had set, and the crest of the low-tide waves took on a near phosphorescent glow. Roxanne Lott loved the beach when it was this way—

deserted and quiet, all the sunbathers gone, the beach-combers waiting for another dawn, the birds away and nesting for the night. She loved it. It allowed her time to think, to ruminate on her life and its future, to plan for the day when she'd be able to leave Assyria and strike out on her own.

And on summer evenings like this, wearing a T-shirt, cut-off jeans, and going barefoot, it was almost as good as making love, without all the sweaty parts.

She stretched her lithe arms over her head and breathed deeply of the salt air; she dropped to the sand and did a dozen quick pushups; she raced her shadow for a brisk hundred yards; she picked up a shell, examined it, and flung it sidearm into the water. A fairly decent toss, she judged, but not one of her best. On a good day she could knock her mother out of the crow's nest with a peanut.

And there was the rub.

The crux of her problems.

The nub of her troubles.

The *TammieRox*.

Many years ago, when she was but a child in diapers, her father had owned half-a-dozen working boats. There were good times. Bad times. Fair times. Lousy times. And now only the *TammieRox* was left, rusting all to hell and leaking from places that didn't even touch the water. Even her dear father was gone, dead these past five years, which left her, her mother, and her younger by a year sister to man the nets, the helm, the anchor, the floppy fish that refused to stay caught, the innards and the eyeballs and the occasional slimy eel that was simply too Freudian to mention.

"It's okay if you want to leave, dear," her mother would say at least once a week, spitting tobacco over the side, not always checking the direction of the wind. "I don't mind. Gonna retire soon anyway, might as well be now as later."

She would sigh then and squint longingly at the sky as if hoping that soon she would join her husband there. Except he wasn't there. He was still here. In the foyer. Wearing his yellow slicker and yellow rain hat, one hand out so his wife could hang her umbrella from his wrist.

Her sister, Tammie, thought it was fun, and had even decorated him last Christmas with spare tinsel and a winking yellow bulb in his mouth.

Roxanne, however, thought it disgusting, morbid, and didn't her mother know the disturbing effect it had on the dates she brought home? Especially when she had to bring out the blindfold?

Dusting him was absolutely out of the question.

She picked up another shell, and tossed it away.

The moon flirted with a thin cloud or two.

Not, she thought glumly, that there were all that many dates to be had anyway in a place like this. Most of the eligible bachelors left town as soon as they graduated from the area high school over in Bally; the rest of them took to the ships, hauling and heaving and doing all kinds of fisherman things, most of which she couldn't abide. Including the sailing. All those waves and floating things and water deep enough to drown King Kong—it was enough to make her shudder just to think about it.

Which, by default, left her home to tend the books, mend the nets, and run the blowfish cake machine in the garage.

And if that wasn't bad enough, now there was Jared Graverly.

For almost three weeks the smarmy real estate man had been making the rounds of every homeowner in town, offering to buy their property for insultingly large amounts of money. In cash. No questions asked, no repairs need be made, just sign the papers and tell me when you're leaving.

"You could be set for life," he had told her just two days ago. "Think of what you could do with all that money. Why, you could go to that college you keep yapping about, you could buy your mother a new car, you could even—"

"Not interested," she'd answered stiffly. She didn't much care for Graverly. Aside from his manner, which was something akin to a slug on speed, he wore blue sharkskin suits, patent leather loafers, and greased his hair straight back from his forehead. Sometimes there were streaks.

"My dear, you shouldn't be hasty. Something like this doesn't come along every day."

Which only proves there is a God, she'd thought.

"I will leave my card. Talk it over with your charming mother and your adorable sister. Neither my client nor I are in any hurry."

But he had been back yesterday morning, and again this morning, each time his manners fraying a little more around the slippery edges. It wasn't right. There was something fishy going on here. Especially when he refused to divulge the name of this mysterious client of his.

Unless it was simply her imagination.

She kicked at the sand.

She was known for her imagination.

Damnit.

Such as, she thought dismally as she booted at a shell along the beach's hard wet apron, the time two years ago when she had thought that the actor who was really a baron and lived in the cottage on the beach at the edge of town had proposed to her. It had been, naturally, a silly misunderstanding, one easily blamed on his accent, all those *r*'s rolling and tumbling and all, but it had had the town giggling at her for months, and the baron avoiding her as if she had the plague.

And like the other time, when she saw the flying saucer land on the north headland, behind the stone mansion. She had seen it clear as day one afternoon, big and round and dropping little green wriggly things onto the ground, which scurried into a hole they burned with a fierce orange laser and were never seen again. So intent was she on taking mental notes for the newspaper that she'd nearly run the *TammieRox* into the rocks at the foot of the cliff.

They had had a good giggle over that one, too.

Then there was the time a while back when a huge white whale tried to—

An idle glance to her left, and she stopped, breath trapped in her lungs.

Oh lord, she thought.

He was there.

Sitting on the sea wall.

Talking to the pirate with the rubber chicken on his shoulder.

A wave of dizziness passed over her, and she swayed.

She didn't know what to do. If he turned around and saw her, he'd probably run screaming into the night, and she'd never see him again; if she turned around and went the other way, she'd end up at his cottage; if she simply stayed here, frozen, and he turned around, he'd probably run screaming into the night; if she stayed here, frozen, she'd freeze her buns off.

She took a step.

He didn't turn.

She took another step.

He didn't turn.

She imagined him spotting her, leaping from the wall, sprinting over the sand to grab her in his arms and declare his love for her at the top of his voice.

A flush crawled over her cheeks.

She rubbed her stomach to calm down.

Rox, she ordered, knock it off.

Another deep breath, a squaring of her shoulders, and she walked unsteadily on, forcing herself to think about Graverly instead, and why his client was trying to buy the whole town. It didn't make sense. Who would want this place?

She stopped again.

The baron?

She looked at him, frowning.

Could it be . . . ? Was it possible? Was the baron the mysterious client? Was he trying to buy the town for himself so he could foreclose on her mortgage and run her out of the state just because . . . nah.

Suddenly the baron gave a yell and flipped backward off the top of the wall.

"Jesus H on a fish hook!" she yelled, when something huge, and very black, flew over her head.

·2·

The large and very black thing soared over the water, banked, and climbed in frustration into the arms of the night.

This wasn't going to work.

Flying around, dive-bombing for meals, had only managed to leave it more hungry than ever.

It would have to think of something else.

It did.

But not before it had thought so much that it didn't watch where it was flying and collided with the towering steeple of the Chapel of Charity, two blocks in from the Atlantic Ocean.

Ordinarily nothing would have happened. The steeple would have collapsed maybe, but nothing more than that. Except that the bells would have melted.

But the flying thing was distracted by hunger and failure, and being distracted, was thus not in full control of itself, and not being in full control of itself, allowed certain objects and events to affect it. Collisions were pretty good at that sort of thing.

Luckily it was able to recover its flight capabilities before it hit the ground, and it slowed down a little, kept its head up and its eyes alert, eventually passing over the local grade school where it could hear the sixth grade choir practicing its little heart out.

Ah, it thought, the children of the night, how sweetly they sing.

It banked, lowered, listened for a while longer, clipped its head against the steeple again, and decided to call it a goddamn night before it found a new way to kill itself.

With renewed strength of purpose, then, it glided straight into the forest that blanketed Nachey Mountain. Its mouth hurt like hell. Not that it could ordinarily feel pain, but it had been a church it had hit, after all, and things like that tended to sting a little when you collided with them.

It landed.

And was instantly reminded that, besides the storms, it also hated landing, especially in the shape it was in, and most especially in the middle of a forest, where it had to hang upside down from a branch right out there in the open, all the blood rushing to its head, everything looking wrongside up and making it nauseous and sometimes cross-eyed. They never mentioned that bit in all the books and movies it had seen, the hanging by your feet and not being able to see straight. It was a poetic license it had long ago decided ought to be revoked.

It blinked.

It sneezed.

The wind rocked it.

It licked around its lips and realized that the fang it had lost that first night hadn't yet grown back, and now wasn't about to.

That was something else they never mentioned—creatures like it had a devil of a time trying to find a good all-night dentist who didn't mind taking payment in kind.

The wind knocked it off.

It hit the ground, shook itself free of the leaves clinging to its wings, took off again and decided to go home, let one of its minions bring it supper, it was tired, cranky, and feeling more than a little peckish.

And it was time, it decided, to stop playing around with these foolish mortals.

As soon as night fell again, it would call its army together and get the show on the road.

It was time to conquer.

– IV –

A Horrible Count (Body and Otherwise)

✦ 1 ✦

The thing about a backward dive, Kent recalled from his childhood days in the Highlands, was to keep those bony knees tucked; not to mention the head. The other thing, because there were actually two things, now that he thought about it, was to be sure there was water down where you were going; otherwise, all those other things being equal, you were probably going to break your neck whether your head was tucked or not. The third thing, thinking about it further since there didn't seem to be much else to do while he was unconscious, was to insure that, if there wasn't any water, at least your bed should be there to help break the fall.

Thus it was that when he opened his eyes and determined fairly instantly by the dull pain at the back of his skull that he wasn't dead, he was not surprised to discover himself lying on his bed.

Some things, like riding a bicycle, you just never forgot.

Other things, however, tended to become bothersome.

For example: how did he get to the bed in his cottage when the last thing he remembered, other than the diving instructions, was that he was on the sea wall and under attack by some mysterious sky creature.

A second example was the rather disturbing fact that, under

the sheet, he was naked, definitely not his condition when he dove from the wall.

A third example of the bothersome, and drifting rapidly toward the nettlesome, was the young man sitting on the armless ladderback chair beside the bed. Neatly dressed and scowling in such intense concentration that his tongue protruded between his lips. He held Kent's right hand. In Kent's right hand was a pen. Beneath Kent's right hand was a sheet of paper attached to other sheets of paper, all of which, to his discerning eye, looked like the pages that made up a contract. The young man was trying to move Kent's hand, and the pen, along the dotted line at the bottom.

Kent stared.

The man muttered and shook his head.

Kent stared.

The man looked up, slowly.

"Jared, lad," said Kent, "have you been talking to my mother?"

Jared Graverly yelped and slammed back in his chair, the papers scattering nervously to the floor.

Kent bunched several pillows behind his back, sat up, arranged the sheet to preserve propriety, and waited for an explanation.

"It's . . . it's not what you think," Graverly explained after a quick, nervous lick of his lips. "I mean, it looks like what you think, but it's not really what you think."

"What I think is, you were holding my hand."

Graverly straightened, insulted. "I most certainly was not."

Kent looked down at his hand.

The real estate agent squirmed. "Well, yes, maybe I was. A little. But it wasn't what you think, even if it looked like it."

I have a headache, Kent thought.

Graverly smiled ingratiatingly. "I was just speeding things up a bit, your lordship, that's all. Didn't want to bother you. I know how busy you are, doing baron stuff and all."

"What things?" Kent asked calmly.

"Why . . . why, selling your house," Graverly replied in surprise.

"And why would I want to do that?"

"Because you said you would."

"When?"

"Last night."

"But as I recall, I was unconscious."

Graverly shrugged. "You muttered a lot. I thought you had agreed to the terms. And very generous ones, at that. You drive a hard bargain, sir, if I do say so myself."

"While I was unconscious?" Kent lifted a hand to forestall further explanation. Instead, he rubbed his eyes, his face, looked around the small, simply furnished bedroom, and wondered what in hell was going on here.

The stone cottage was a basic four rooms with fireplace, and two sets of sliding glass doors leading from both the living room and the kitchen to the patio. A slate roof in fine repair. A garage to the left from which the doors had been stolen some years ago, along with the car inside. The nearest house, and the true beginning of the Assyrian residential zone, was a brisk fifteen-minute walk north. The beach directly in front of the flagstone patio was not so much sand as boulder and rock, seaweed and disgusting slimy things, which prevented day-long accumulations of shrieking children and pot-bellied fathers from disturbing his peace; although it also ruled out sexist displays of barely covered female flesh, more's the pity.

This deliberate isolation had been further assured by his subsequent purchase the following year of three hundred contiguous acres of prime Maine soil and all the stuff that grew in it. Indeed, the woodland across the road had also been posted against hunters and trespassers, thus serving as an amazingly crowded but well-mannered refuge for creatures on the lam from shooting-and-stuffing season.

And it sure as hell wasn't for sale.

"Jared?"

Graverly sat up like an eager puppy. "Sir?"

"Bugger off."

He pointed to the door.

The young man sputtered.

Kent augmented the severely pointing finger with the equally severe aristocratic look that had, in its time, banished everyone from uppity servants to a tax collector who had climbed over the battlements in a wet suit.

Angrily, Graverly bounded to his feet, gathered the fallen papers into a briefcase, and stalked out. Returned and said in a voice much too solemn for one of his tender years, "You will not escape his notice, you know."

Kent blinked. "Whose notice?"

"The Count's."

"I'm a baron," he said.

"But he's not. He's a Count."

"Who?"

Graverly smiled evilly. "The Count."

He left, not quite slamming the door behind him.

Kent stared, scratched through his abundance of quiet ginger hair in more than a thatch of bewilderment, then tossed the sheet aside and proceeded to get dressed. His head still hurt. His stomach muttered something about food and where the hell was it. And he was bothered by the fact that Graverly had managed to get into his house without his knowing it. That he was, at the time, unconscious, somehow didn't seem to matter.

When he opened the bedroom door, he heard voices low and animated coming from the front of the house.

Hello, he thought; did I throw a party and forget to go?

Cautiously, in case the smarmy young agent had decided not to leave after all and was practicing another clever sales pitch for the comatose, he moved down the short hall into the living room, and stopped.

On the overstuffed couch set perpendicular to the fireplace on the lefthand wall was Roxy Lott. In the overstuffed armchair set opposite the couch was Dick Walker, the Assyrian chief of police.

A glance at the sliding glass doors told him, by the marked absence of sunlight, that it was dark outside; by the feel of the air, he could also tell that a storm was brewing; by the sound of the constant surf, the storm was very close; by the clock on the mantel, he knew it was just past nine.

When the pair finally realized he was there, they looked at him with a combination of *thank god you're alive* and *oh dear*, and there was an awkward silence. Then, rubbing her hands together eagerly, Roxy scrambled to her feet, said, "You must be hungry, starving, I'll get you something, sit down," and ran out of the room.

Bemused, Kent watched her leave before moving carefully to the couch, sitting, and pushing himself into a corner. He smiled at Walker.

The chief jerked a thumb toward the kitchen and said, "You barons have all the fun."

Kent sneered without rancor. Dick was a good man, a tall man, a heavy man, a supremely impressive man in his gold-and-black uniform with little green pine trees sewn onto the breast pockets and on the sides of his thigh-high black riding boots. As such, then, the policeman seldom had any trouble with miscreants, and what trouble he did have seldom lasted for more than a minute or two, and most of that was spent by the cowering offender apologizing for remarks undoubtedly made about the size of the chief's nose. Which in itself was supremely impressive, more so because it was accentuated by bushy eyebrows over tiny eyes and a handlebar mustache sweeping down around a mouth whose lips were basically thin to nonexistent. He wasn't ugly, wasn't plain, and never went hunting for moose in the fall.

"So," said Walker, "how do you feel?"

"Like hell."

"Happens when you fall off a wall."

Kent crossed his legs. "Just for the record, Dick, I didn't fall. I was brutally attacked, and jumped out of the way to save myself. I just happened to be seven or eight feet above the ground at the time."

The chief nodded thoughtfully. "And what, sir, attacked you?"

Kent didn't know and admitted it. It was big, it was nasty, it came out of the sky like the Red Baron except that it was black, and it had knocked him to the beach.

Walker nodded again, then explained that Roxy had been coincidentally jogging along the beach at the time of the incident, had seen the big black thing herself, had seen the baron fall, and, with Claw Tackard's able if clumsy assistance, carried his lordship back to his cottage where she had looked after him once the doctor had ascertained that there was nothing so seriously wrong with him that a day of rest and recuperation wouldn't take care of it.

Kent glanced at the doorway. "She did that?"

"Beats making blowfish cakes."

He rather supposed it did, although he wasn't sure he liked having his recovery expressed in such nautical-cuisine terms. He inhaled slowly, rubbed a thoughtful hand over his chest, and gazed around Walker's chair to the almost stormy night beyond. "And what about Graverly?"

"He was worried about you," Roxy said, returning with a tray of plates, cups, saucers, toast, butter, jams, buns, tea, scones, two bagels, and a large orange with a bent straw jammed into it. She set the tray on the low table between them, hesitated before sitting beside Kent, and began to parcel out the food and drink. "I didn't think he would be so stupid."

"Was born stupid, Roxy," Walker said with a fatherly chuckle. He looked at Kent. "I suppose he tried to get you to sell your place?"

"In a way."

"Did you?"

Kent shook his head.

Roxy handed him a cup, a plate, and pointed at the food. "Eat," she commanded. "Doctor's orders."

He ate.

He drank.

He listened while the chief complained about Graverly trying to buy up the whole town, and not having a whole hell of a lot of success doing it, all in the name of some mysterious foreign person who had taken up residence in the stone mansion on the headland. The real estate agent was evidently driving everyone nuts, and had marked himself as a prime candidate for a lynching if he didn't knock it off soon.

The wind began to blow.

Whorls of sand spun across the flagstones.

Kent's stomach ceased its culinary protests, and he relaxed with a silent, contented sigh, stretched, and noticed that Roxy was looking particularly fetching this evening in her red-check hunting shirt opened one too many buttons down, black jeans, and bare feet.

Bare.

He blinked. Once. Slowly.

"You've been here . . ." He dared not bring himself to say it. "All this time you've . . . the bed . . . my . . ." He dared not think that Roxy Lott, of all people, had—

She blushed.

Be damned, she had.

He blushed.

He stammered a thank you for looking after him.

She muttered a you're welcome, it was my pleasure, then blushed so hard her eyes went bloodshot.

Kent chewed rapidly on a slice of toast.

Roxy chewed ferociously on a buttered scone.

Chief Walker chuckled himself into a coughing fit that ended when he saw the expression on Kent's face.

Time passed.

Kent studied the fireplace. "I, uh, do have pajamas, you know."

Roxy rolled her eyes. "I found them. They have pictures of smiling, hairy cows on them."

"They are Highland cattle," he corrected stiffly. "And they are not smiling."

"The cute little flowers are."

"Heather," he replied, just as stiffly.

She grinned at him.

The wind rose.

"And I like my pajamas, damnit," he muttered.

Another silence, during which Chief Walker stepped to the brink of hysterical giggling, and eased back with a grunt and a grab for a scone.

"They have flaps," Roxy whispered.

"Jesus!"

Walker choked on the scone, and she hurried to his side, pounded his back several times, and patted his shoulder when he signaled, with a groan, that he was fine, thanks, leave my spine alone, it helps keep my head up. She patted him once more for good measure before returning to the couch, this time curling up in the opposite corner.

Kent finished his tea, the toast, the rest of the scones, and was absently peeling the orange when he wondered aloud if the chief was here on a social call to the recently, not to mention most viciously, wounded, or was it a business call as the result of a mysterious message sent to Kent only a few days ago. He smiled then, because he knew that a man unconscious for twenty-four hours or so would never receive a business call from the police.

"Business," Walker stated. "No message."

Right, Kent thought; right.

The chief cleared his throat in obvious embarrassment.

Kent began to have another one of those damned feelings, and he was fairly positive it wasn't because Roxy had seen him in the all-together since that was, of course, purely in the realm of good neighbor relations, give the baron a hand, lass, he's knocked himself silly, don't matter if he's starkers.

He blushed.

Walker cleared his throat again.

The wind thumped against the glass doors.

The suspense, Kent thought, is putting me to sleep.

"He wants to ask you about Purity Horton," Roxy blurted.

"Never touched her," he answered quickly.

"I know," Walker said, with a glare at Roxy. He cleared his throat a third time. He stared glumly into the fireplace.

"She's dead," Roxy told him.

Oh lord, he thought; open mouth, insert foot, ankle, and half your bloody knee, lad.

He leaned forward, hands clasped between his knees. "An accident?"

"Maybe," the chief replied flatly. "As best we can reconstruct it, Buddy Plimsol dumped her on the Ledge three weeks ago, after they had an argument. Drove away and left her. She walked down on her own. Something must have frightened her, she tried to take the shortcut." The chief looked at him. "You know the shortcut?"

Kent smiled innocently. "I've heard about it."

Roxy humphed.

He ignored her.

The policeman took a deep breath. "She must have fallen. After that, we don't really know anything. Except," he added, "that she bled to death."

Kent shuddered. Bit into the orange, spit out the straw, put the orange down, and waited for the rest of his visit to be shot all to hell.

Walker glanced at Roxy, then coughed into a fist. "We . . . that is, I . . . that is . . . oh hell, sir, I don't know. I need your help!"

I knew it, Kent thought.

"That's the sixth mysterious death or disappearance this month."

I knew it, I knew it.

"All the same. The deaths, that is."

I knew it, I knew it, I knew it.

"So tell me," Walker said, plucking at some stubbornly invisible lint on his chest. "How's your mother?"

Kent looked at him.

"How's the cottage, everything all right?"

Kent looked at him.

"Had any orgies lately?"

Kent looked at him.

"So, how many punctures does a vampire leave, one or two, I keep forgetting."

Heaven's Path wasn't a very large or very fancy cemetery. It was, more than anything, practical—a simple waist-high fieldstone wall topped by seven-foot iron-spear fencing, a single high and ornate iron gate so perfectly counterbalanced a child could open it with a gentle push, old trees and carefully mown grass, and tombstones whose dates were as early as Seventeen and Forty-five. A handful of plain, copper-door mausoleums clustered near the back. A few angels both in repose and upright, a fair number of cherubs, the occasional lamb and faithful dog and a single dove of peace on the wing. It faced the seaside town from the barely noticeable lower slope of Nachey Mountain; behind it was a dense and deep forest of pine and fir and enough oak and maple to make autumn a joy.

A place for serenity and meditation.

A place for coming to quiet terms with one's mortality.

Buddy Plimsol, on the other hand, felt lousy.

First, the chief of police had questioned him near to death about what had happened between him and Purity; then his mother had insisted that he at least make an effort to visit the poor girl and try to make amends.

He was, after all, the last person to see her alive.

So, drawing on the dip and gulp of Dutch courage he had had at the MooseRack, he aimed his flashlight at her newly minted headstone and tried to think the right thoughts, feel the proper respect, dredge up a little guilt, and, at the same time, ignore the fog that crept around the bases of the trees, swirled around the graves, curled around his ankles, and made him feel as if he were sinking in wet cotton.

"Well, hell, Purity," he finally said, "that was a pretty dumb thing to do."

Not exactly, he figured, what his mother had in mind, but what was he supposed to do, fling himself on the grave that hadn't even settled yet and bawl his eyes out? He'd ruin his clothes, for god's sake.

He stood for five minutes more, shifting his weight from foot to foot, thinking about having another tall one or two at the bar, and trying to decide just how much respect you were supposed to show a dead person who didn't know you were there in the first place, and who'd probably cut your balls off if she did know, because he'd dumped her.

Man, he thought, dying is hell.

The wind picked up.

The distinct scent of rain in the air.

A light tap on his shoulder.

He whirled in a terrified panic, fell over the grave that hadn't even settled yet, and jabbed his flashlight in front of him as if it were spear.

"So," said Purity Horton, "you doing anything tonight?"

He gasped.

She laughed.

And behind the next tree, a wolf began to howl.

"How many holes does a vampire leave," said Kent calmly.

Walker squirmed.

A brief flash of distant lightning over the water.

"A vampire. In Maine."

Walker tugged at an earlobe.

"Dick," he said, "we have known each other for a long time. Even though you still haven't found out who stole the doors off my garage, I respect you as a fine police officer, a generous human being, and a gentleman. Come to think of it, you haven't found the guy who stole the car that was in the garage at the time either, but I do not hold a grudge. I understand the pressures. I know how it is to be in the public eye. So please do not be offended when I say, with all sincerity, that you are out of your effing bloody mind."

The wind blew.

The sand scuttled.

The lightning came closer, dragging thunder with it.

"All the deaths," Walker continued desperately, "were the same."

Good lord, Kent thought; an Assyrian serial killer.

Jesus.

"They all bled to death, just like poor Purity," Walker continued without prodding. "Or, they were all drained of their blood anyway. Not a drop left in their pathetic little bodies. Weren't none on the ground where they were found neither."

Roxy shuddered and shifted closer to Kent.

Kent's stomach felt a little queasy. "I'm sorry to hear that. Very sorry. I . . . but why are you telling me? What's all this nonsense about—"

"Roxy has a theory," the chief said, for some reason not wanting to meet his gaze.

Kent didn't ask. He knew about Roxy Lott's theories. He remembered all too well that silly misunderstanding some years ago that had made her the laughing stock of Assyria for months, but for his part, all had been forgiven. On the other hand, there was the other stuff. Like the whale, and the elephant's skateboard, and that pulsing maroon glow under the water out by the buoy.

Then, without thinking but putting two and two together and coming up with bananas, he said, again, "A vampire."

Thunder.

Lightning.

Roxy slapped his shoulder and pointed triumphantly at the policeman. "Damnit, Dickie, I *told* you!"

"Damnit, girl, there were no marks!" the chief countered, nearly shouting.

"Hey," Kent said.

"There was no blood!"

"Hey," Kent said.

Walker's face reddened. "They didn't have no holes in their necks!"

"They had one!"

Kent made to say *hey* again, but instead said, "One?"

Roxy looked at him in triumph, putting a finger to the side of her neck. "Right here. I saw three of the victims with my own eyes."

He sniffed. He wasn't sure but he thought he heard the patter of rain on the roof. He took her hand and said, gently, "Roxy, I understand that you are sorely upset, and confused because of the tragedy visited on this town of yours. But a vampire—dear lord, I can't believe I'm talking like this—a vampire leaves two marks on the neck. Two. One for each tooth."

"Then where the hell is the blood?"

More lightning.

More thunder.

Lots of wind blowing stuff around.

"C'mon, Baron, let's hear it," she challenged. "All you have to do is tell me where the hell all the blood went."

At that moment the lights went out.

Roxy uttered a short but conclusive scream.

"Bloody hell," Kent muttered. He got to his feet and made his way to the mantel from which he took a thick white candle. Walker handed him a lighter. The wick flared. Shadows crawled over the walls.

Somebody knocked on the front door.

Hot wax dripped on Kent's hand, making him swear and drop the candle on the hearth.

It went out.

Someone knocked on the front door.

"I'll get it," Roxy said.

Kent waited as she crawled off the couch; he looked down as she fumbled around his shoes; he looked up when somebody knocked on the front door.

"I thought you were going to get it."

"I meant the candle. You think I'm going to answer the door in the middle of the night in the middle of a storm when there's a vampire knocking off people left and right?"

She has, he thought, a point.

"That's my ankle," he said a moment later.

"Vampires," muttered the chief of police, "don't leave one mark on the neck."

Kent decided that what remained of his sanity would be best served by going to the door himself. That way, Roxy wouldn't be messing around with his ankles—although he had to admit she had a nice touch—and he wouldn't have to hear anymore about Dracula and such. A thought that made him chuckle quietly as he barked a shin against the coffee table on his way out of the room and up the hall. It was probably Graverly, thinking he'd gone back to sleep; or it was his agent, lugging a hell of a wonderful script for a Broadway play that would, at the very least, put his name back in lights; or it was, he thought, frowning as he opened the door, two tough-looking women in ill-fitting trench coats and kerchiefs, one carrying a gnarled walking stick taller than she was, the other a bronzed shovel.

"Lordship, we got trouble," gasped Lavinia Volle.

"Purity Horton," gasped Frieda Juleworth.

The wind tore at the cottage.

Lightning streaked toward the top of Nachey Mountain.

"I know," he said, standing aside. "Won't you come in?"

Lavinia gasped again. "You know?"

"Told you," Frieda told her. "These movie stars know everything before it happens. I see it all the time."

Lavinia waved her stick. "But we just saw her!"

Kent smiled, gesturing them inside before his hair blew off. "You do fine work, I'm sure."

"She was messing around with Buddy," Frieda said, leaning on the shovel.

"Once a slut, always a slut," Lavinia said.

"Ladies, ladies," said Kent, swinging his arm in the hope that they would get the message and get the hell in out of the storm, "don't you think a little charity is in order here? The poor child is dead."

"Don't I know it," Lavinia snapped. "Damn near broke my back digging that damn hole."

Frieda smiled apologetically. "Strained it when we was pulling a stump two weeks ago," she explained. "These things take a while to heal, you know."

"Ladies," Kent implored, "please come inside."

Lavinia leaned forward, squinting. "She in there?"

Kent blinked. "Who?"

"Purity Horton the slut," Frieda said.

"She's dead."

"She's a slut," Lavinia muttered as best she could over the howling wind, the lightning, and the thunder.

"Who is?" Roxy demanded, stomping up the hall.

"Purity Horton," Lavinia answered.

"Well, sure she is," Roxy agreed, shouldering Kent aside. "But she's dead."

"That's what I told them," he said.

"But if she's dead," said Frieda, "how come we just saw her?"

"You dug her grave," Kent reminded her.

"You . . . just . . . saw . . . her?" Roxy gasped.

Wind.

Rain.

Kent wondered if he could nudge Roxy over the threshold and close the door without anyone knowing.

Lightning.

Thunder.

His feet were getting wet.

Lavinia pounded her walking stick on the stoop. "You gotta do something!"

She was right.

"In!" he bellowed. "Damnit, get in here! Now!"

The women squealed and hustled through the doorway, shovel and stick at the ready, eyes fearful and wide.

Kent slammed the door.

The storm stopped.

The lights went on.

As Roxy herded the chattering gravediggers toward the living room, promising them food and warm drink, he stared thoughtfully at the door. Opened it.

Lightning.

Thunder.

He closed it.

The storm stopped.

Pursing his lips in a *don't ask* tuneless whistle, he slipped his hands into his pockets and followed the others to the front room, where Dick, always the proper gentleman, had risen to greet them, to listen politely to their incredible story, and to head for the sideboard where he poured, unasked, two large tumblers of Kent's private stock of Glenbannock. He drank one as Frieda explained how she had spotted Purity floating down Mercantile Lane, moving away from the cemetery toward Beachfront Avenue; he drank the other while Lavinia allowed as how it certainly appeared to her to be an impossible circumstance unless one considered the girl's reputation, the storm, and the mysterious Count who had taken over the unnamed deserted mansion on the headland and had once been seen, fleetingly, walking the streets, muttering ominously to himself.

And, Frieda added, let's not forget his beautiful assistant.

Kent leaned against the mantel.

Not to mention, Lavinia reminded her, the little fat guy with the pointy beard who claims to be a professor.

Walker dropped into the chair and stared balefully at his empty glass.

"So," the two gravediggers said to Kent, "what are you going to do about it, lordship sir?"

"My second-best friend was one of those victims," Roxy whispered, moving to his side. "And her . . . poor little sister."

Of course, Kent thought as she took a long, slow, incredibly ridiculous deep breath revealing too many emotions for one man to absorb, I do not for a minute believe any of this. Yet, he thought further as she took another long, slow, incredibly ridiculous deep breath, there was obviously something horribly wrong with Assyria this night, or Dick Walker, ordinarily a down-to-earth fellow who wore gloves when he had to clap for

Tinker Bell, wouldn't have mentioned any of it. But he had. And people were dead. Or missing.

Roxy squeezed his arm.

He looked at her; he looked at the two women; he looked at the chief of police; he looked at his reflection in the sliding glass doors, which told him that he was, once again, out of his goddamn mind for even thinking about trying to get out of this in one piece.

"What," he said at last, "do you want me to do?"

Roxy sighed. Deeply.

"Never mind," he said quickly. He frowned in intense concentration. He scowled in fierce internal debate. He rubbed his jaw and tugged at an earlobe and pulled at his nose and lightly massaged his neck. "I think," he said, "the best thing will be for you, Dick, to take these two ladies to the cemetery and see if anyone has been at Purity's grave."

"She ain't there," Frieda muttered.

Kent ignored her. "Roxanne, hie yourself to your home and change your clothes. Get some shoes. We may have a lot of walking to do before this night is done."

Roxy moistened her lips.

Kent ignored her. "I myself will go to the MooseRack and talk to Freddie and Mabel. I will meet you all there in an hour's time."

He waited.

Walker pushed himself out of the chair and pulled on gleaming black gloves, set his braid-trimmed black-and-silver cap onto his head, and nodded once, sharply.

Roxy moistened her lips.

He waited.

No one moved.

"Well?" he said.

Roxy handed him his denim jacket and, with a sweet smile, said, "After you, m'lord."

Damn.

·2·

Professor Tarkingdale parked his rented car on the side of the road, just past the entrance to the marina, where the main road made a sort of shrimp fork split, the narrow righthand tine heading straight up a low rocky rise onto the flat-top headland.

Up there, he was now positive, was his nemesis, living high off the hog with electricity and everything, and no one to bother him because that rocky road would easily take the stuffings out of anything but a tank.

If he was going to get it over with tonight, he would have to walk.

Thank god for the weather.

He lit his pipe, cranked the window down a little, and let the smoke drift out to be shredded by the wind. What he needed was a little luck here, some foresight, and about forty pissed-off peasants with torches and hay forks and half a brain among them. What he had, however, was about forty fishermen whooping it up at the MooseRack, at a birthday party for the local mortician; he also had an assistant who insisted on attending that party so that she would better be able to infiltrate the good graces of this village; and a plan that, he thought as lightning took out a hickory, needed a little work.

Perhaps he should retire to his room and muse.

He nodded.

Yes. Absolutely. A capital idea. It would be supremely foolish of him to attempt to face the nefarious enemy on his own, without any accurate knowledge of the size of its hellish following or the intricacies of the mansion's no doubt twisting and endless dank corridors.

That would be suicidal.

Once, many years ago, he had nearly gotten killed tracking the Hawking Hell Hound of Babylonia through a very similar structure, whose dank and dusty halls didn't seem to lead from one place to another. It had only been good fortune, and a fairly decently cultivated loud hailing voice, that had brought his assistants racing to his side. But not Dianna. She had been in the village, infiltrating. He meant the other ones. The poor unlucky souls who had been dragged to shrieking perdition by the Hawking Hell Hound's slavering jaws before Sloan had been able to drag the painstakingly prepared herbs from his briefcase and send the beast whence it had come.

His suit had been ruined, too.

No, he thought as he refired the ignition and swung the car back in the direction of town; no, this time he would be fully, completely, and absolutely prepared.

The engine sputtered.

Something white and frilly drifted across the road in front of him.

He braked without thinking, the engine coughed, and the storm broke directly over his head.

Blast, he thought angrily.

When the automobile refused to move again, he checked the dashboard and slapped his forehead in professorial chagrin. Out of gas. How in the name of everything he held dear and holy could he have forgotten to fill the gas tank? But there was no time for acrid recrimination or pondering the cruel coincidences of a merciless Fate. Hastily he locked all the doors, opened his pampered leather briefcase, took out his weapons du jour, and settled down to wait. Sooner or later, someone would come along to rescue him; sooner or later, the storm would end and he could safely walk the few blocks back to his hotel without ruining his suit.

Meanwhile, he would be vigilant, alert, and prepared for anything the enemy could devise.

Assuming the damn garlic didn't do him in first.

Dwight Lepeche examined the raspberry jam and assorted fried beetles on the gold-rimmed platter set before him in the massive dining hall of the stone mansion, and shook his head in gloomy resignation. He dared not refuse the meal, dared not question the Voice's explicit orders, but deep down inside, where a shred of decency clung for dear life to what remained of his immortal, if scruffy, soul, he had to admit that this "Yes, Master" business was beginning to bug him.

"You've failed me," the sexually charged voice declared sadly.

"I don't know," Jared said. "I thought it was pretty good."

She slapped him.

He gaped.

She slapped him again.

He stumbled backward.

She took an angry step forward.

He looked around frantically for some kind of protection, but there wasn't much to see in the middle of the beach in the middle of a storm, wading as he was in the water.

She glared. "I will have to do it myself."

"But it wasn't my fault he woke up!"

The storm illuminated her incredibly ethereal, yet downright earthy, beauty.

"You must concentrate on the girl instead."

Well, it could be worse, he decided; she could have told him to tackle the graveyard twins again.

Lightning danced around her.

Thunder bellowed above her.

The waves boiled around their knees and nearly knocked him off his feet.

"We *must* have that land, Jared," she reminded him for at least the dozenth time in the past hour. "Without it—" She stopped herself abruptly, picked up a blanket floating by, and wrapped it sensuously around her shoulders. "Tomorrow," she warned. "If you do not do this one little thing by midnight tomorrow . . ."

He knew it.

As soon as that damn naked baron woke up, he had known he was doomed.

Well, if she thought he was incompetent, that he would fail the ultimate test, she had another think coming. As she undulated elegantly out of the water and disappeared into the dark, except when there was lightning, he vowed to her marvelously turned back that she would eat crow before the sun set again.

He raised a fist in determination.

A wave knocked him over.

He crawled to the beach and raised the fist again.

A wave knocked him over.

He crawled to the wall, looked behind him, raised a fist, and laughed.

Tomorrow, he declared firmly in silent but anticipated triumph; the sun will come out tomorrow, and you, lady, can bet your bottom dollar that tomorrow, I, Jared Graverly—

A wave knocked him over.

"Shit."

Eddie Salem, a state-honored teacher of English and Early Renaissance Woodshop at the regional high school over in Bally, stood impatiently in front of his undeveloped property at the south end of town and wondered if Jared would be stupid enough to give him a full million for it. The last time they had spoken, the offer had gone to seven hundred fifty big ones. It was, considering the amount, only a small jump to six zeros as far as he was concerned.

He sniffed.

He scratched his buttocks.

He noted that the houses across the street, and on either side of his property, were dark. Had they been sold? Were their former owners already lounging in Florida and Arizona, telling their new neighbors of the horrid New England winters, the rocky soil, and the insects many believed had been trained by the Luftwaffe? Were they already rich?

He sighed; it didn't matter. He had long ago stopped wondering why this mysterious Count person on the cliffs wanted so much land. If the guy was willing to pay for it, it wasn't for Eddie Salem to question him, not if his check was good and the IRS didn't know.

He glanced up at the night sky, and pulled the collar of his hunting jacket closer around his neck, tugged his cap lower over his brow.

He checked his watch.

The little prick was late.

Something moved, back there in the trees.

"Jared?"

A flash of white between two birches.

"Jared, damnit, that you? Get a move on, eh? It's gonna rain, and I'll catch pneumonia out here."

A figure drifting toward him.

Eddie frowned, then straightened.

It was a woman.

He squinted, checked the deserted street, and looked back into the trees.

She stopped just shy of coming out into the open.

"Eddie," she whispered.

He blinked. He rubbed his knuckles over his eyes, stared, and blinked again. He couldn't believe it. "Wilma? That you, Wilma?"

"Eddie," she whispered huskily.

He took a step closer. "Wilma Popper?"

No, he thought; it couldn't be.

She stepped into the open.

By God, it was!

Wilma Popper. Little Wilma Popper. Class of '88, if memory served. Slim, graceful, large blue eyes, and always wearing some sort of baggy camouflage outfit to prove her declared solidarity with the trampled masses of some country or other. Class social rebel. Never seen without a petition in one hand and a chewed cigar in the other. Close friend of Roxanne Lott, who Eddie had always put in the front row in case one of her father's shirts popped open.

"Wilma," he said, puzzled but pleased, "we missed you at the class reunion last June."

Wilma fluttered her eyelashes at him.

Then Eddie realized that the nightgown she was wearing wasn't camouflaged at all. In fact, in the strength of the post-storm moonlight he could see just about everything he hadn't been able to see in the four years he had taught her how to use a lathe and a power drill. Nuts, he thought.

"Eddie," she whispered seductively.

He smiled rakishly. "So. What brings you back to Assyria? I haven't seen you since your funeral."

She lifted her arms.

He checked the street again.

"Eddie," she said.

He smiled.

She smiled.

He stopped smiling and said, "Funeral?"

She smiled wider and said, "Power to the People."

And the last thing he thought as she wrapped her arms around him was, *staples, they look just like great big staples.*

Dwight Lepeche belched.

All in all, with a little chocolate sauce, it wasn't half bad.

Then his head cocked, he frowned, and threw down his napkin. "Oh nuts, tonight?"

The wind whistled through the mansion.

"Really?"

The sea pounded the base of the cliffs.

"On a full stomach?"

Dianna Torne was bone-tired and ticked off. Her feet hurt, her eyes hurt, her brain hurt. From virtually the first second of their arrival in Assyria, she and the professor had been making the rounds of all the shops, restaurants, bars, official buildings, and the one behind the local stable that had a pink light over the door, all in an effort to track the whereabouts of *his* lair.

And all efforts had thus far ended in complete, frustrating failure.

It wasn't that they weren't asking the right questions, or that they hadn't, by the judicious planting of cash on seemingly fertile ground, gained the confidence of the townspeople; they had.

And it wasn't that she hadn't been able to work her womanly wiles on the male population; she had.

It was just that nobody was talking.

Oh, they crossed themselves a lot and made the hasty two-finger sign that supposedly warded off the evil eye, but other than that, they refused to cooperate. It was almost as if they were afraid that their lives would be in mortal danger were they to speak to strangers of that which was, by its very nature, unspeakable.

Which, of course, they were, and it was; but still, it was a pain in the ass.

Now she stood in front of R BINGHAM & SONS, FUNERAL DEPOSITORY in what she perceived would be her final chance at locating *his* secret hiding place. A term that was, she decided as she opened the squeaking gate in the picket fence that bordered the large well-kept corner yard that set the pre-Revolution-style building back from the sidewalk, rather stupid. If it's a hiding place, then it's secret. If it wasn't secret, why bother to hide there? In fact, she continued as she mounted the wide brick steps and rapped on the double doors, if you were there, you really wouldn't be hiding, would you? You'd just be waiting around for someone to come along and get you. So it wasn't even a hiding place, much less a secret one.

The door opened.

She found herself face to face with a woman who, by the look of her, was either an incredibly old hag with the most beautiful white hair in the universe, or a desiccated middle-age woman whose absolutely stunning hair had gone prematurely white. She was also thin, bony, and wearing a black velvet dress with white lace about the neck and cuffs.

"Yes?"

"I'm looking for R. Bingham," Dianna said, trying to see over the woman's head. "I was over at the bar"—she pointed to MooseRack, on the lefthand corner—"and they told me I'd find him here."

"That's Rowena," the woman snapped crustily, "and you've found her."

Dianna did not gape, neither did she gasp, nor did she sputter and stutter. After all, she was a seasoned fighter of Evil, and nothing threw her anymore, not even aged Victorian women who ran funeral parlors. Quickly, then, before her composure faltered, she explained who she was. Miss Bingham, instead of asking questions, backed away and gestured her inside, through a large reception area filled with potted palms and into an office furnished primarily by a desk that could have doubled as a barracks in an unexpected civil war.

Miss Bingham climbed into the seat behind it; Dianna sat in a leather armchair facing her.

Miss Bingham folded her hands on the blotter.

Dianna smiled.

Miss Bingham stared.

Dianna heard a truck rumble by outside.

Miss Bingham stared.

Finally, Dianna could stand it no longer: "I'm sorry, Miss Bingham, forgive me, but I'm afraid I was expecting a male funeral director."

"Undertaker."

She frowned slightly. "That's what I said."

Miss Bingham shook her head. "Nope. You said 'funeral director.' Ain't. You think I stand on a coffin and move people around with a baton?" She laughed into a powdered palm. "Cue the trumpets, Gabriel, got another one on the way?" She laughed again and pulled a silver flask out from a drawer, screwed off the cap, poured a drink into a glass shaped like a lavender liver, and sipped. "Young lady, I ain't a funeral director or a grief counselor or a pre-internment product supervisor. If they're dead, I either plant 'em, burn 'em, or, like I did for Captain Lott just a few years ago, mount 'em. But that was a special case. A bitch, too. Kept falling off the pedestal." She sipped again, offered the flask, and raised a plucked eyebrow at the slow shake of refusal. "Anyway, what can I do for you? There's a party for me next door and I don't want to be late."

Oddly enough, Dianna relaxed. She knew this woman wouldn't be the slightest bit impressed with the usual spiel, the appeal to basic human nature, the petition for understanding that which is, by its very nature, un-understandable.

So: "Miss Bingham, have you had many inexplicable corpses around here lately?"

The undertaker stared at her as if she hadn't heard a word. Then, with a sip straight from the flask, she pushed herself out of her seat and wandered toward a high curtained window that overlooked the main street.

Dianna rose and followed; she knew she had struck a nerve.

"Have you spoken with the police yet?" Miss Bingham asked.

Dianna shook her head.

"Did you shake your head?" Miss Bingham asked, parting the curtains with one trembling hand.

Dianna nodded.

"Did you just nod?"

She did it again.

Miss Bingham pointed outside.

Dianna looked over the woman's head.

"Lot of dead folks out there," the undertaker said quietly.

Dianna knew it was true; she'd seen livelier towns after sunset in Transylvania.

Silently they watched a barrel-chested man with a clawed pegleg hobble by, with a rubber chicken on his shoulder. He played a battered concertina; and the tune, Dianna realized with a shiver, was somewhat ominous in a jaunty sort of way.

As he faded into the shadows, Miss Bingham said, "I am eighty-six years old today, you know. Eighty-six. Been running this place for forty of them, ever since my father dropped dead." She looked over her shoulder at Dianna's chest, blinked, and looked up. "Not one of them bodies ever got the notion to visit relatives again. Until last week."

Sweat broke on Dianna's palms.

"Of course, it's poppycock," Miss Bingham continued. "Dead people don't walk unless they weren't really dead in the first place. Which, if they weren't when they died, they were when I got through with them." She making a sucking sound with her lips. "Embalming and all."

Dianna nodded.

A car backfired smokily to the curb and a raucous group of men piled out and whooped into the MooseRack. She thought it an odd place for a bar, though she imagined that the sight of Miss Bingham's establishment practically next door tended to keep a lot of rowdy drunks sober.

Miss Bingham turned back to the window.

She pressed two fingers to the side of her neck. "Right there," she said.

Dianna whipped out a diamond cross from around her neck and held it up.

Miss Bingham sighed. "Each one of them had a peculiar mark right here." The fingers moved. There was no mark. But Dianna quickly deduced what the woman meant.

"I see."

Miss Bingham spun around. "Good lord, really?" She ran to the desk and took a mirror from a drawer. Checked her neck. Frowned. "Ain't nice to fool an old lady, young lady. Especially on her birthday."

A man strolled up the street from the south. As he passed in and out of the light, Dianna noted that he wasn't all that bad in an aristocratic sort of way. The best thing, in fact, that she'd seen since coming to this miserable place.

"The mark," she said, watching the man pause to peer somewhat warily at the sky. "Didn't anyone else notice it?"

The undertaker refilled her flask from a bottle hidden in a bust. When she'd rebuttoned her dress, she wandered over and poked her head around Dianna's arm.

"The only one who said anything was Reverend Ardlaw."

Of course, Dianna thought; the clergy is always alert for the presence of Evil.

"What did he say?"

"He wanted to know what the mark was." Miss Bingham snorted. "Said I wasn't doing my job. 'Course I was doing my job. 'Course again, it was easy. Ain't hard to embalm when you don't got blood to take out first."

Dianna gripped the windowsill tightly. "And what did the doctors say was the reason for that?"

The undertaker cackled. "Doctors? We don't have doctors in this town, miss. We got specialists. Up the old you-know-what. They said the folks died of massive blood loss. Wasn't their job to figure out where it went."

"Fools," Dianna muttered.

The man in the street looked around indecisively, scratching the back of his head.

Miss Bingham parted the curtain and squinted, then nodded. "Nice, huh?"

Dianna looked down at her.

"Ain't every day we get royalty around here, you know."

Dianna's heart stopped. "Royalty?"

"Sure. Lives all by himself just past the edge of town. Nice guy, though. Real bear with the ladies, if you know what I mean."

My god, Dianna thought; the absolute gall and nerve of the man! Walking around in broad moonlight! Making friends! Having dinner! What the hell kind of fiend was he?

Calm yourself, she ordered; be professional.

"Have you . . ." She cleared her throat when her voice began to crack. "Have you noticed anything unusual about him?"

"Well, not really. He does talk a little funny, come to think of it. Bought a lot of land. Nothing special, though. Why?" A woman-to-woman nudge of an elbow. "You interested?"

"Oh yes," said Dianna Torne solemnly, nodding. "Oh yes, indeed."

·3·

Roxy pedaled home as fast as she could. It wasn't that she was afraid of what might happen to her, although she admitted that she really didn't want to end up like her second-best friend and her sister; it was just that she had to change, wash her hair, do her nails, and make sure that her one decent dress hadn't been left draped over the blowfish-cake machine. She seldom had a chance to wear it, and tonight she was determined to make a good impression, to convince the Baron that she wasn't the ditz he thought she was.

Not that he had call to point a finger, what with those smiling cattle flap-pajamas and all.

Nevertheless, this was her chance to redeem herself, and she wasn't about to blow it.

As soon as the chief had muttered something about things coming to a head, coming to a boil, only beginning, this was only the start, Kent had taken charge so manfully, so powerfully, so impressively, that she'd almost swooned. His plan was masterful. The only thing about it was, she already knew what he was thinking before he even talked to the Hortons.

He thought they were all crazy.

But he hadn't seen her second-best friend, Wilma Popper, and her poor little sister, Cornelia, lying there so serenely in their matching pink coffins, Miss Bingham's skillful work cleverly disguising the telltale mark of the vicious vampire that stalked their tiny community.

The very creature that had nearly gotten her out on the beach.

For, not long after she had left the cottage, she remembered the big black ugly thing that had nearly taken off her head and had subsequently introduced her to a side of the Baron she hadn't seen before. Purity probably had, she thought uncharitably, but she sure hadn't; and from what she had seen, she wanted to see more.

Hence, the dress, the hair, the makeup, and all the rest; and thank god her mother and sister were in Portland, attending a protest against the outlawing of one-man submarines used in the herding of fish toward the nets.

She pedaled furiously.

Water dripped from the leaves, the eaves, the telephone wires.

The clouds were gone; the moon had risen.

She slowed as she passed the Dining Salon and Bar and saw Kent walk inside. She wondered how he'd gotten there so fast, and decided that royalty had its own way of moving about mysteriously, in the night.

She passed a car parked at the curb three blocks farther on, and saw the fat little professor sitting at the wheel. Nothing else. Just sitting. She wondered why he was sitting there, and decided that academics had a life the ordinary fisherwoman was not privy to.

She passed the well-lighted entrance to the marina, swung a sharp left across Beachfront and up a short, dead-end lane to the end.

Her home—a tiny Cape Cod, comfortable and paid for, and just big enough for three, unless she counted her father in the foyer, which she didn't.

She left the bike on the porch and hurried inside, muttered something to her father, and ran immediately into her bedroom. Thirty minutes later she ran out again, cursing, nearly weeping with frustration because all she had to wear was a snug shirt that once belonged to her father, a snug pair of jeans, and tennis shoes with lightning stripes along the side. How the hell was she going to make an impression dressed like that?

Someone knocked on the door.

Stomping angrily past her father, she peered through the curtained pane and saw a man on the porch.

A tall man.

An aristocratic man.

A devilishly handsome man in a tuxedo, with a red-lined opera cape tossed casually about his broad shoulders. His hair was dark and brushed straight back from his forehead, but unlike Jared Graverly, there were no grease marks on his brow.

He bowed slightly, smiled.

She gulped.

He mimed a request for her to open the door.

"Who are you?" she called nervously.

He smiled.

She knew she shouldn't do it. He was a stranger, she was a woman; he was handsome, she wasn't bad; he was virile, she was panting; and then there were his eyes. Dark eyes. With a hint of red in the center, but not without a certain amount of Old World charm. Beckoning eyes. Promising eyes.

Commanding eyes.

Her hand reached for the doorknob.

He smiled.

And somewhere in Assyria, in Maine, a dog whispered a howl.

·4·

There were a number of reasons why Kent liked the MooseRack Dining Salon and Bar, foremost among them being it was the only restaurant and drinking establishment in town that didn't have lobster cages and old fishing nets hanging from the beams, forty variations of cod on the menu, and crooked oil paintings of storm-tossed sailing vessels on the walls. Instead there were glassy-eyed moose heads, deer heads, beaver heads, woodchuck heads, and a stuffed buzzard over the kitchen door. The light was dim enough for privacy in the booths along the wall, the bar was well-stocked and inexpensive, and Freddie Horton was about the best cook he had ever met.

Unfortunately, he hated to go inside.

The first time he had done so, many years ago, he had fallen back against the wall and shouted, "Damnit, Mother, how the bloody hell did you track me down here!"

It had taken five strong men and Mabel to convince him that no one had ever dreamed that his mother in full battle gear resembled a rearing, snarling polar bear, especially one with an arrow through its head from temple to temple.

Usually, then, in order to preserve his appetite, he closed his eyes when he walked in, not opening them until he'd made an abrupt right turn into the dining room.

Tonight, however, he was no sooner across the threshold than Freddie himself took him roughly by the arm and virtually dragged him left, into the crowded bar, and to an empty booth near the back wall, beyond which was a redwood terrace currently occupied by a gang of young people obviously determined to see who'd be the first one to throw up on the grass below.

Kent held his temper at the unaccustomed treatment. After all, there had been a tragedy in the Horton family not long ago, and Freddie was no doubt still upset over his daughter's demise. He noted instead the streamers, balloons, and the buffet table set in the middle of the floor; he noted as well that the place seemed unusually crowded. Birthday? he wondered; anniversary?

"I want you to kill Purity," Freddie demanded as soon as they were seated and Kent had taken off his jacket.

Kent waved to Mabel behind the bar, and she nodded as she moved to pour him a drink.

"Did you hear me?"

Kent had, and was at a complete loss how to respond. Grief was something he only dealt with on his continuing daytime drama; and as a butler on said program, there wasn't an awful lot of emoting to do. Not that he hadn't tried. Emoting by not emoting was a hell of a trick. Too bad the director hadn't agreed, the little twit.

He smiled politely.

Freddie ran his hands through his tightly curled hair and leaned over the bare table between them. "You think I'm nuts, right?"

"Freddie, I—"

Horton hushed him with a chop of his hand.

Mabel hurried over and set a glass down. "Did you ask him?"

"I did," Freddie said.

"What did he say?"

"He ain't said nothing yet."

She turned to Kent, who turned his polite smile to her. "Are you going to kill our Purity or not, your lordship? We haven't got all night, you know."

I am, he concluded, missing something here. Dick had left out the stuff about mass hysteria. He decided then that this was no time to tell them that their daughter had been spotted not more than an hour ago. He suspected, in their state, they'd try to form a lynching party.

Somewhere on the other side of the table-crowded floor, and beyond the dance floor, someone played a menacing sea chantey on a screechy concertina.

Mabel scooted her husband over and sat down. Her round face was flushed, her salt-and-pepper hair somewhat frizzled, the print dress she wore much too dowdy, he thought, for her usual genial nature. She picked up his glass and drained it. Freddie shook a cigarette from a pack and lit it from a lighter that doubled as his tie clip.

They exchanged what Kent hoped was not a meaningful glance.

Mabel smiled. "Maybe," she said, "we didn't put it exactly right."

"Maybe," Kent suggested, "you ought to start from the beginning. But," he added with an upraised cautionary finger, and thinking about the bizarre meeting he had just left a while ago, "let's leave out the vampires, the walking dead, the wolves, and the mysterious man who's got so many of you so obviously terrified out of your minds."

They looked at him.

He looked back, patiently.

They looked at each other.

He tried to get the bartender's attention.

They looked at him expectantly.

"Well?" he said. "Don't you have anything to say?"

Freddie stubbed his cigarette out on the table. "You told us not to talk about vampires, the walking dead, the wolves, and the Count."

Kent straightened, remembering Graverly's threat. "The Count? Who's the Count?"

Mabel fussed a handkerchief from the depths of her bosom. "You told us not to tell you."

"We're only trying to help, you know," Freddie snarled sullenly. "We're not used to dealing with people like you."

"The Count?" Kent said.

"Yeah, him too."

"But who is he?"

Mabel began to sniffle.

Freddie pushed back into the corner and sulked.

After due consideration, Kent suggested gently that perhaps the overwhelming and overpowering sorrow of their recent bereavement had somehow twisted things so that they did not look like what they thought things looked like, and they would all look better in the morning.

Mabel sobbed.

Freddie sulked.

An elderly woman with incredibly beautiful white hair and a Victorian dress, and wearing a cone-shaped paper birthday hat, came up to the booth, said, "Ain't my fault, you know," and walked away, blowing on a plastic horn.

One of the young people on the deck began to scream.

Kent leaned over and patted Mabel's hand, suggesting in his best comforting voice that if she wished, he would personally see to it that the beast that had done such a terrible thing to her only daughter would rue the day it had come out of the woods. He also suggested that Doc Jones, who had at that moment entered the bar with a woman on either arm, might have a little something in his bag to help her sleep tonight. Then, tomorrow, he, Kent, would come over and they would all see how things looked so much better than the way things had looked the night before.

Freddie glared at him.

Kent decided a break was in order. He smiled at them to remain where they were, slipped out of the booth, and made his way to the bar. As he ordered another drink, a thin man to his left with thinning grey hair and a handsome lean face looked up at him and said, "The drapes."

Kent smiled blankly.

"Just mind the drapes."

"I thought it was the other thing," a man to Kent's right said.

Kent looked.

The man was pale, his long hair parted in the center, his lips quivering, his face not as lean as the other man's but lean enough to be called lean.

"Pardon me?" Kent said.

"The other thing. I thought it was the other thing you had to mind."

"No," said the first man. "I ought to know. It's the drapes."

"Damn," said the second man. "You're right. I've been thinking about the electricity stuff."

"Ah."

"Yes."

Kent picked up his glass.

The thin man on his left took hold of his arm. "Just remember what I said. If I don't know, nobody does."

"Well, Chris does," argued the second man.

"Oh. Yes. I forgot."

Kent escaped, thinking as he returned to the Hortons that he'd just been told something vital, and something stupid, and right now was in no mood to figure out which was which.

He sat.

He smiled at Freddie, who scowled back at him.

"Maybe," Mabel said to her husband, "we should have talked to the Count."

"What Count?" Kent asked.

"Too late now," Freddie replied bitterly, waving his cigarette toward the deck glass door, where the screaming young man was now trying to yank it open. "Son of a bitch can't hold his liquor."

"Who?" Kent asked. "The Count?"

"Marty Elegra."

"Marty Elegra's a Count?"

Freddie stubbed his cigarette out on the table and pointed to the redheaded kid pounding frantically on the pane. "That there is Marty Elegra."

Kent looked at the kid, looked back at Horton. "I know that. His father's a butcher. I just didn't know he was a Count."

Horton closed one eye. "He's not. He's just a kid, for god's sake."

Kent closed both his eyes slowly. Opened them slowly. "All right. All right. The kid pounding on the door is not a Count. The Count is someone else. Who you will not talk about because I said you weren't supposed to."

Freddie nodded emphatically.

So far, so good, Kent thought.

"Which part?" he asked fearfully. "The vampire part, the wolf

part, the walking-dead part, or the man who's frightened you all
to death part?"

"Yes!" Mabel wailed.

No, he thought.

Freddie held up one finger. Kent watched as if hypnotized as
the restaurateur brought the finger to the side of his neck and
jabbed at it. Just as Roxy had. "Right here, your lordship," the
man said, with an angry catch in his voice. "She had the mark
right here!"

"The . . . mark."

He was beginning to think that being nuts was catching.

The kid pounding on the door suddenly began weaving and
ducking and batting at the air, along with all his friends. Doc
Jones yelled at him to stop that damn obscene dancing or he'd
call the kid's father.

Mabel blew her nose. Swiped a hand under her eyes to banish the tears. Leaned forward and whispered, "The mark of the
vampire."

"Ah."

For a moment, one he thought he'd never have in his life, he
wished Roxy was here with him. Her kind of nuts he was used
to; this was getting a little deep, even for Assyria.

The Victorian woman walked back over and said, "Except for
Mabel's daughter, when I do 'em, they stay done," and walked
away, blowing on her horn.

That woman, Kent thought, has been sniffing the casket
linings again.

He turned back to Mabel. "All right. I think I understand
now."

"Told you he would," Mabel said smugly, and patted Kent's
hand.

"But will he do it, is what I want to know," Freddie wanted
to know.

"Do what?" Kent asked.

"Kill Purity, of course," Mabel reminded him.

"Who had," he said, very slowly, "the . . . mark of the . . .
vampire . . . on her—"

"Yes!" she cried.

He looked woefully at his empty glass. "And who, if you

don't mind my asking, explained that this was the mark of
the . . . vampire?"

Freddie pointed to the wall. "Tarkingdale."

Kent looked at the wall. "And he's . . . the Count?"

"Oh Jesus," Horton snapped. "Don't be a—"

"Freddie!" Mabel cautioned. She lowered her voice again.
"He's a professor, your lordship."

"Ah. Yes. He's been mentioned. Then . . . who is the Count?"

"Beats me," Freddie answered.

I will not lose my temper, Kent told himself; I will not lose my
temper.

"All right," he said.

And leaned back in shock when Freddie bellowed, "For
Christ's sake, will you stop saying that and just go kill my
goddamned daughter?"

The room fell quiet.

A woman began to sob.

The glass door shattered inward.

Roxy opened the front door.

"May I . . . come in?" the tall, handsome, aristocratic stranger
asked in a voice as deep as the ocean, as high as the night sky.

She almost nodded.

He smiled.

She saw his teeth—straight and white and glinting a little in
the moonlight.

One, however, was missing.

"May I . . . come in?"

Roxy screamed and slammed the door in his face.

Professor Tarkingdale started the engine of his rental car and
drove as fast as he dared to the hotel. He parked. He scrambled
out. He ran inside and puffed up the stairs, divested himself of
his garlic necklace, his garlic ear plugs, and his garlic headband,
grabbed the cross he had had made from emeralds on a Pacific
island lost only last year to a rampaging volcano god—through
no fault of his own, god knows he had tried—and changed his
clothes. Then he raced back down the stairs and puffed up the
street. He would have to find Dianna, tell her that *he* was in the

mansion, and ask her what she thought they ought to do next.

Actually, he knew what to do, but it was his experience that a second opinion was always helpful in matters like this.

Besides, she had always been better at gathering the peasants; for some reason, they never trusted him. He suspected it was jealousy, not only for his erudition and manner, but also his clothes. Peasants never had clothes like his. They always had peasant clothes. That's why they were peasants.

A loud screaming stopped him.

Up the street a crowd of people poured out of a bar, yelling, shouting, waving at the air. At the same time, he spotted Dianna Torne pushing her way through a squeaking picket fence gate on the corner. Without a moment's hesitation, he hurried up to her, grabbed her arm, and said, "Something's afoot."

Dianna agreed. "I think it's . . . *him*."

The concertina sounded its deepest note, barely heard above the running and shouting and yelling and waving.

Tarkingdale agreed. "And I know where he is."

"So do I."

They began walking slowly toward the mob.

"You do?"

Impossible. She was wrong. He was the professor, and he knew where *he* was. A glance to his left. How could she find out where *he* was, in a funeral parlor?

The crowd settled a little, although three men ran around the corner and up the street and through a gate in a high stockade fence. They were carrying guns.

"Fools," Tarkingdale said. "Don't they understand what they're dealing with?"

"No," said Dianna.

Gunshots.

Shouts of alarm.

More gunshots.

Tarkingdale didn't flinch.

Dianna slapped his shoulder and pointed. "There!"

He gasped, and reached for his garlic, remembered that he had left it back in the room, and reached for his emerald cross. "Where?"

She pointed again. "There!"

He blinked. "That man is *him*?"

Solemnly she nodded.

"But he has a rubber chicken on his shoulder."

She slapped him again. "Not him. Him!"

He saw a moderately tall man, fairly muscularly built without being ostentatious about it, a disgusting amount of dark ginger hair, and a face that, in other circumstances, might have appeared on a stoic but highly educated butler. The man moved among the crowd, speaking softly, calming them, touching them, smiling, nodding sympathetically and nodding again. Within minutes, the crowd, and the man, had returned inside.

Dianna ran a smoothing hand over her dress, through her hair, across her eyebrows. She took a deep breath. "Wait here," she ordered.

"But Dianna," he protested, "shouldn't we just use the stake and be done with it?"

A gentle pat to his cheek. "You're forgetting his minions, Sloan. We may destroy *him*, but unless we destroy the minions as well, *he'll* be back. As *he* always comes back when his minions survive."

Tarkingdale saw the size of the man, and the wisdom of her conclusion. He whispered that he would check the goings-on in the back, and suggested that she use her womanly wiles on the Count to get him to reveal all.

"Exactly," she agreed.

Tarkingdale smiled.

She kissed his cheek in farewell, and he held his breath as he watched her walk forth to do battle with the enemy.

The poor bastard, he thought gleefully, doesn't have a chance.

There's a little brown church in the wildwood, and a little brown church in the vale, but neither of them had the Reverend Laurence Ardlaw as their pastor; his was the medium-size white Chapel of Charity out on Pineneedle Road, six blocks in from the main street and one short block south of Heaven's Path cemetery. The rectory beside it was modest and clean, and at the moment the clock struck ten o'clock, it felt awfully lonely.

The tall burly cleric stood at his living room window, hands clasped loosely behind his back, and gazed out at the street shin-

ing with the recent rain. There was no one out, despite the fact
that the evening was mild, and he could see no lights in any of
the houses.

They are afraid, he thought sadly and compassionately; truly afraid of the great Evil which has been unfairly visited upon
them, afraid of the Devil's Own Servant who walks among them,
afraid of seeking Comfort where Comfort should be most obviously sought.

With him.

And Him, he added hastily, lest he be thought to have
indulged in the vice of Pride. Unless it was a sin. He was
never really clear about any of that. Vice, sin, it was all the
same to him, and the Lord knew he had partaken of both during
his wastrel youth, before the Call had come and he had cast aside
worldly things to take up the Cloth and march with other stalwart
Christian soldiers against Evil, the Devil's Servants, and all that
other stuff.

He sighed.

It was, however, difficult to march when the band had already
gone the other way and around the corner.

Not, he amended guiltily, that Assyrians were bad people.
They weren't. Give them a good hurricane or a radical change in
fish migrations and they packed the Chapel to the rafters. It was
just that when they were faced with the supernatural, somehow
God didn't seem to fit in.

His hands fluttered about his black lapels, fluttered to his
embarrassingly bald head for someone so young, fluttered to
his sides and twitched there for a while.

He sighed again and tried to figure out what he should do
next. Not long ago, in order to cloak some charisma about him,
he had attended a week-long seminar in Bangor and returned
with his head polished. Not clean. Polished. Something to do
with self-image. He couldn't remember exactly what, now. But
it had helped for a few weeks, and never had his sermons been
so well-received or so powerfully delivered.

But tonight all that seemed for naught.

Lord, he prayed, give me a sign that I, Thy humble Servant
not of the Evil type, may take up Thy Standard and carry it
forth before the Legions of Thy most of the time Faithful; give

me a sign that I may bring Strength and Salvation to these Thy
fisherpeople, and the butcher.

The doorbell rang.

Reverend Ardlaw grinned.

The doorbell rang.

He hurried into the vestibule and opened the door.

"Good evening," said a tender feminine voice. And even
though she stood in shadow, visible only as if seen through a
subtly shifting gossamer veil, he could tell immediately that she
was, unquestionably, a beautiful woman. A tempting woman.
A gorgeous woman with long ash blonde hair and a figure that
Larry hadn't seen since he couldn't remember when, but it was
definitely before he had cast aside all his worldly belongings
and joined the Good Fight. Thank you, God, he prayed, for not
making me a priest.

"Yes?" he said with a broad, welcoming smile.

"My name," she said, "is . . . Belinda Durando."

His heart fluttered as his hands fluttered. He stepped aside.
"Won't you come in? Miss Durando?"

She came in.

She brushed past him.

His hands fluttered.

His pate blushed.

She turned in the foyer and said, "I believe my good friend,
Jared Graverly, may have mentioned me?"

Larry swallowed several immediate and intemperate re-
sponses. Jared had indeed mentioned her. Several times. Several
detailed and excruciating times. Several detailed, excruciating,
and damn disgusting times. The cur. If the greasy little real estate
agent had been a member of his congregation, Larry would have
slapped him, and forced him in penance to fix the steeple, which
kept getting involved in mysterious nighttime collisions with
oddly shaped nightbirds.

"Yes," he breathed. "I do believe he has." He smiled regretfully. "And I am afraid that this property is not for sale."

Belinda Durando smiled. "I do not want your property, Reverend."

He nearly lost consciousness.

"It is, in fact, you I seek."

He leaned against the wall and hoped she wouldn't notice how his knees refused to lock.

"Reverend—"

"Larry," he said quickly. "Please. Call me Larry, or Reverend Larry, or Rev Larry—that's what the teenagers call me—or Laurence, or L.A., or Pastor, but please don't call me Reverend. It's so . . . formal."

She smiled.

He returned the smile.

She said, "I believe . . . Laurence . . . that you are acquainted with Mr. Kent Montana?"

"The Baron?"

She nodded.

He nodded.

She nodded. "I have been trying for several days to contact him, but I'm afraid . . ." Her arm spread to indicate helplessness, though such a condition evidently did not extend to her support garments.

Larry cleared his throat several times to mask his impending disappointment. "And you need an introduction?"

She nodded.

He nodded. It figured. Gorgeous women were hard to come by in this town, and they all went by Montana's place, even when he wasn't there, which was most of the time. His right hand fluttered to his neck. It must be the collar. And the black suit. Maybe I should dress like a Presbyterian, or one of those TV guys.

He glanced at the heirloom grandmother clock in the hallway leading to the kitchen, then nodded toward the living room couch. "If you'll take a seat, Miss Durando, I'll call and see if his lordship's at home."

"Oh, but he's not."

Larry frowned. "He's not? How do you know?"

Her smile wavered. "I'm sorry. Larry. I thought you meant the Count."

"The Count?"

She nodded.

He nodded. "Ah. Yes. The gentleman from the headland mansion who has the whole town buzzing." He walked with her to the couch, but remained standing as she sat and crossed her legs; and he wondered how such a short woman could have so much leg. "I had forgotten he was a Count."

"He is."

"Well, his lordship's not, and if you'll excuse me, I'll see if he's at home." He grinned conspiratorially. "The Baron, not the Count."

Her smile returned fully formed. "Wonderful. And afterward, perhaps you can tell me all about this . . . lovely town of yours." She smoothed a hand over her grey wool knit skirt. "If, of course, you wouldn't . . . mind."

He smiled an *of course not, I'd be delighted, think nothing of it* and hurried into his study, closed the door, checked the telephone book, dialed the baron's number, and hung up after one ring. The man, he thought, really should learn to answer his phone more quickly. Then, with no feelings of guilt at all, he hurriedly took off his collar, his jacket and rolled up his sleeves.

He smiled to himself.

Larry Ardlaw—tall, bald, burly, and a sucker for blowfish cakes—was nevertheless no fool. He knew that he was the most prominent religious figure in Assyria, and as such and by default, it was natural that he become the most tempting target for the Servants of Evil. And Belinda Durando was a Servant if he ever saw one. He sniffed, rolled his broad shoulders to shed some tension, and sucked in his stomach. It was going to be a long night, and a tough one, but he fully expected that one more pitiful soul would be saved by morning. And since his lordship would be saved as well, even if he didn't know he was going to be saved, Larry was positive the man would know how to show some true Christian appreciation. Maybe, he thought as he patted his pate with a sheepskin buffer, a new altar, a new car, or a repair job on the steeple.

As he opened the door, somewhere outside, a small dog began to howl.

He smiled.

They had taken a long time getting around to him.

They would find that *they* had, at last, met *their* Match.

Then he saw the grey wool dress folded neatly on the coffee table, and Belinda Durando unfolded on the couch.

Oh boy, he thought; this one's gonna be a bitch.

·5·

Chief of Police Dick Walker stood silently at the foot of Purity Horton's grave and noted with practiced eye and some twenty years of investigative criminal experience that nothing had been disturbed, except for the divots where Lavinia had tripped over her shovel and claimed that a hand had reached out of the ground to grab her. No; all was as it should have been—the earth hadn't been moved, the headstone remained upright, and fresh flowers had been placed in a nearby stone vase.

Lavinia sneezed.

Frieda muttered a "God bless you."

Lavinia replaced a divot and whacked it one with the shovel.

The chief ignored them.

By all rights, relief should have been his. Having done his duty, he should have been able to hurry straight back to the MooseRack and inform the baron that all was well in Heaven's Path, everybody seemed to be home, no one had left a forwarding address. Consequently, he should have been able to tie one on and forget Roxy's dumbass theories even if he had been tempted for a while there to believe them himself, what with the holes and no blood and all. After which, or probably before which, he should have been able to go to his office next to the bait-and-card shop and call the state cops and let them handle the murders, then head for the pink-light district for a little rest and recreation.

Unfortunately, such was not his fate.

"Damn," he said.

Carefully hitching up his uniform trousers so as not to soil the two-inch cuffs, he knelt beside the waxen body of Buddy Plimsol lying beside the grave that hadn't been disturbed, and noted with forensic detachment that the kid was pretty dead. He also noted that there didn't seem to be a mark on him of a violent, and therefore life-threatening, nature. A gesture brought Frieda's flashlight closer.

"Lord," he whispered with a shake of his head.

The expression on Buddy's pale and drawn face was one of complete surprise, mingled with a touch of terror, which suggested to him that the boy hadn't expected his demise. Either that, or he hadn't expected the demise to have been caused by whoever or whatever had caused it.

"You gonna check?" Lavinia asked.

He glanced up at her, annoyed.

"Don't worry. He twitches a finger, I'll crop him one with the shovel." She smiled sheepishly. "I had Reverend Larry bless it this afternoon. Just in case."

The chief decided he had nothing to lose, and so, using a stick because he didn't want to disturb the evidence or touch a dead body, he turned Buddy's grass-matted head gingerly to one side. To expose the neck.

Frieda aimed the flashlight.

"Damn," he said again.

One hole, just over the jugular vein.

And one quivering drop of blood.

Aside from the residue of the storm, the ground around him was completely dry.

Frieda squinted, and scratched her neck thoughtfully. "You figure he's using a straw, or what?"

·6·

All right, thought Kent, all right. Let us assume for the nonce and the moment that all this nonsense isn't nonsense at all but the diabolical forerunner of an invasion by a creature so foul in folklore and legend that nobody believes it. Let us further assume that we do, as a matter of fact and for the sake of current argument, believe it. Let us next assume that, having believed it and, now that we think about it, having actually been attacked by it, we have to do something about it before Assyria, and Maine, as we know them, exist no longer except in folklore and legends that nobody believes.

The question is: do I give a damn? Will I, in the still of the night, as I gaze out my window, be able to sleep with a clear conscience? Well, not if I'm staring out the window, but let's assume that I'm sleeping instead. Will I be able to? Or will I be riddled by lurid nightmares, haunted by wailing ghosts of former friends and acquaintances, stalked by the blood-drained specters of those I could have saved if I had, from the beginning, given a damn? Could I introduce this guy to my mother?

He kicked his heels back against the sea wall, looked down at the beach and kicked again.

Damn, but he hated moral dilemmas.

On the one hand, girding his loins to help save the town—

and there was, he reminded himself glumly, no guarantee that he would be successful—would be the *right* thing to do. It's what heroes in the movies always did, and they never thought twice about it. They just marched right out there without a qualm, grim but determined, filled with vim and vigor, shirt open to their navel and not a hair out of place. Of course, they had a script to follow. Nobody ever asked them what they really thought, which was probably that only a flaming idiot would stick around to fight nasty immortal things that sucked your blood and turned you into the living dead and could transform themselves into bats and wolves and who the hell, as it were, knew what. I mean, what kind of jerk would stick around against odds like that?

On the other hand, he wondered why in hell there was always another hand. It never clarified things; it only complicated them, and was a pain in the neck besides. He grunted. Bad choice.

Roxy straddled the wall easily to his left, a light pullover sweater tied by its arms around her waist.

He looked at her sourly, looked back to the sea as it tried to claw the beach into oblivion.

A chilly wind tugged at his hair, made him flip up the collar of his denim jacket and stuff his hands into his pockets.

So far, actually, he hadn't done too badly for whatever it was he was supposed to do. He had calmed the patrons of the MooseRack when those kids had been assaulted by, they had claimed, a trio of truly ugly bats driven away by the subsequent further assault of Freddie Horton and his trained shotgun; he had not throttled Roxy herself when she claimed Bela Lugosi had tried to get into her house and she'd broken his nose with the front door; and he had noted before being dragged away by a grateful populace an extraordinarily beautiful woman who, he was later told, was Professor Tarkingdale's assistant. The professor himself was the little fat guy with the goatee.

But what, he asked himself, did that add up to?

What, truly, had he accomplished.

Not, in the scheme of things, one heck of a lot.

He puffed his cheeks and sighed.

The sea in sympathy grumbled back at him.

"Listen," Roxy finally said. "You don't have to do it, you know."

He grunted.

"I'll understand. Really. This isn't your town. You don't owe anybody anything, and it wouldn't be fair to ask you to put your life on the line for folks you don't owe. Not here. We're nothing to you, not really. Just some quaint Down East fishermen you like to look in on once in a while, have a few laughs with, and be on your way to exotic places where you can meet rich and beautiful women. I understand. Assyria isn't even on most maps. Why should you care? I mean, really, we all know that you have your career to think of, and if you get involved with something like this, it could ruin you. I know that. And nobody would blame you if you just packed your bags and left on the next bus. Really. We can take care of ourselves. We've been doing it for generations, and no . . . no *creature* . . . no *monster* . . . is going to stop us from carrying on. So you don't have to worry about offending us. We know. We understand. And we won't think less of you. Really. No kidding."

He looked at her.

Her lips tried to form a brave smile.

"Okay," he said.

She blinked. "What?"

He shrugged. "Okay. I'll leave in the morning."

She hit him.

He fell off the wall.

She jumped down beside him, grabbed his coat, and yanked him to his feet, and glared at him, nose to nose. "Over my dead body!"

He grinned. "I think you've ripped my jacket."

She glowered.

He told himself he would probably regret this tender moment for the rest of his life, give or take a few days, and he kissed her.

She kissed him back.

Maybe, he decided, not.

Two heads poked tentatively over the wall. One of them was a rubber chicken, unless it was a dead vulture; the other belonged to a pirate. "Is this where I play the romantic stuff?" Claw asked hopefully.

"No," Kent told him.

"Damn. I got a good selection, too. Lots from Italy and Spain, exotic foreign places like that." Then he looked regretfully at his vulturine shoulder ornament. "It's the claw, ain't it, sir."

Kent blinked. "What?"

Claw shifted, and propped the cleverly carved claw of his pegleg atop the wall. "Argh, the claw. Puts people off, don't it."

Kent marveled at the pirate's dexterity and looseness of limb.

"It belonged to me parrot."

Roxy released Kent's coat. "What?"

"Me parrot." Claw smiled sheepishly. "Well, actually, it really didn't belong to me parrot, what died these twenty years ago in a bar fight back in Morocco. It's just modeled after his foot." The smile faded and he caressed the ivory-and-teak claw lovingly. "He was a good old bird, he was. Argh, and very romantic in his way."

"Claw, I realize that—"

A siren blared deafeningly on the street.

Startled, Claw snapped his head around to see what was going on, cried "Whoops!", scrabbled frantically for a grip on the wall, and failed; pirate, bird, and claw flurried, flailed, and finally yelped from sight. A moment later, the sound of a pained concertina drifted over the sand.

Another siren whooped.

The concertina wheezed.

Kent dashed along the beach to the nearest stairs, Roxy keeping pace behind him, and climbed to street level just in time to see the flashing lights of a speeding ambulance swerve around a far corner, closely followed by a police cruiser. He crossed the band of grass to the curb. A small group of people had once again left the MooseRack and, down to his right, the Lobster Is Inn, as well. Cigarettes were lit; someone called to someone else poking a head out a window.

This, Kent realized glumly, is what's known as foreboding.

Then he spotted Dick Walker stalking determinedly across the road toward him, his snappy black riding boots reflecting the streetlamps in their thigh-hugging depths. His cap was square, his gloves tight.

Kent didn't like his expression; this is what's known as I don't want to hear it.

Roxy muttered something he didn't catch and untied her

sweater, slipped into it, muttered again.

Claw untangled himself rather noisily from the concertina and readjusted Bruno.

The night turned chilly.

When the chief finally reached them, he rubbed his gloved hands together and shook his head. "Two more," he said simply. "Buddy Plimsol. I found him in the cemetery. Next to Purity's grave."

Roxy gasped.

"And Eddie Salem. He was found on the sidewalk in front of his undeveloped property."

Roxy gasped.

"And the marks?" Kent asked, because he couldn't help himself, he was that kind of baron.

The chief only nodded.

Good, Kent thought sourly; the next thing you know, folks will dash for their homes, lock the doors and windows, and start hunting in the attic for the family Bible.

Suddenly Beachfront was filled with people again, racing for their cars, their pickups, a couple of motorcycles in an alley; gunning their engines, shouting, backfiring, and speeding away into the night. Within minutes the street was deserted. It was quiet. Neon winked out. The slam of a door echoed over the town. Across the way, downstairs lights flared on in Rowena Bingham's establishment.

Wonderful, Kent thought; just . . . swell.

He felt Roxy tremble a little beside him, and tried one of his blatantly false, albeit game, reassuring smiles. "You know, lass, the way things are going, all we need now is a little fog to spook things up."

She gaped. "How . . . how did you know?"

"Know what?"

"That," said Chief Walker portentously, and pointed with a black glove.

Kent resisted for at least twenty seconds before looking behind him. And there, just beyond the thundering breakers, he saw a low wall of writhing grey creeping toward the beach. He frowned suspiciously, glanced up the street, and said, "Not to mention the—"

High on the pine-choked eastern slope of Nachey Mountain a wolf howled.

"Oh great," he muttered, jamming his hands into his jacket pockets. "So what's left? The—"

Something large and black flapped slowly overhead.

"Now cut that out!" he snapped.

Tackard played a single deep note reminiscent of a cathedral organ.

"You too!"

The pirate shrugged—*hey, I'm only doing me job, sir.*

Swiftly the fog swept soundlessly inland, crawling over the sand, the wall, and into the streets. It wasn't thick, but sufficient to make the buildings across the way blur at the edges and set a haze around the streetlamps.

"I don't think we ought to stand around here too much longer," Walker suggested. "Considering the deaths and alleged vampires and all, it might get a little dangerous in a little while."

"Aye," Kent replied. He checked the street again, and remembered what Freddie Horton wanted him to do. Good lord, he thought in a sudden minor revelation, you don't suppose . . . "Claw, do me a favor and take Miss Lott to the SurfSide and book her a room for the night."

"Hey, wait a minute," she protested. "I can take care of myself, if you don't mind."

He shrugged. "I don't mind."

"Damn right."

"But do you really, and I mean really want to sleep in your own home tonight?"

"Damn right."

"Alone? In the dark? After being visited once already? By a guy who's probably rather annoyed that you smacked his nose with your door? With no one to help you in case you need help? Alone?"

She gnawed lightly on her lower lip.

"I'll pay," he offered.

She grabbed the pirate's offered arm. "Lead the way, Captain."

He smiled. A plucky lass, but not terminally stupid. "We'll meet in the morning."

"I suppose you have another plan?" the chief asked without bothering to disguise a skepticism that was, by the same token, not to be taken personally.

"Of course. Tomorrow, rain or shine, we're all going to pay a surprise visit on the Count."

Walker took a surprised step backward and fell off the curb. "The Count? Are you nuts?"

"If," Kent said, "he is what you think he is, and I'm beginning to think that he is too, then he'll be helpless during the daylight hours, if I recall my legends and folklore correctly." A glance toward the headland showed him nothing but fog. "Perhaps we can end this quickly."

"You think so?" Roxy said hopefully.

Not a chance, he thought.

"Sure," he lied.

Claw reached for his concertina. She slapped his hand away, and warned him to mind the claw, it was gouging her sneakers all to hell.

As they left for the hotel, vanishing by ghostly stages into the night, Kent turned to the chief. "You have some business, I would imagine, with bodies and such, Dick, so you'd best take your own advice and get about it."

Walker saluted. "A long night, sir, ahead of us."

Kent nodded.

"What are you going to do?"

"Me? I'm going home, get some sleep, make a big breakfast when I wake up, make a few phone calls, then meet you all here in the morning."

"You're a brave man, sir," the chief said as he saluted again and moved away.

Kent smiled modestly at the man's back. Then he frowned. "What do you mean?"

The man walked on. Into the fog. Bootheels loud on the black-top.

There were no echoes.

"I mean, going home. Alone. No neighbors to help you. No one to hear you scream. All those dark woods across the road, empty beach on either side." His voice faded. "There are them's who might think you're out of your mind."

He vanished.

And Kent stood alone. In the fog. Listening to the breakers. To the buoy's sad ringing. To a foghorn's forlorn cry far up the coast.

Sonofabitch, he thought; why didn't I think of that?

The fog swirled.

A garbage can lid rolled and clattered in an alley.

"Hey," Kent called.

There was no answer.

Kill my daughter, said Freddie and Mabel Horton.

"Dick?"

We're all going to die, paraphrased the message.

"Nuts," he muttered. "Hell."

Then someone, or something, tapped him on the shoulder.

The large white-and-green lobby of the SurfSide Hotel was primarily extraordinarily healthy rubber plants and white wicker furniture, sturdy carpeting, and squared posts behind which tourists were able to indulge in a bit of lurking now and then to spy on the other tourists to see what they were doing and why they were having more fun than the lurkers. By midsummer, the manager had to post a schedule; by summer's end, there were always a few spares.

Thus was Professor Sloan Tarkingdale able to take advantage of chair, plant, and squared post to keep an eye on the entrance, just in case *he* came calling. Tarkingdale wouldn't put it past him. Once *he* knew he was in the neighborhood, the battle would be joined, and he wouldn't be surprised if *he* made a preemptive strike on his home base just to keep the professor off-guard. It was why he and his assistants usually never stayed in one place for more than a few days at a time. Things tended to get messy when the *he*'s of the farflung Evil Empire of Evil got their backs up.

Since leaving the commotion downtown, however, nothing had happened. For which peaceful interlude he was grateful. Not, he thought as he gingerly parted a rubber plant to check the front desk, that he wasn't worried about Dianna. After all, she was a valuable addition to his team, even if she was damned expensive. But his concern lay more in the area of overtime rather than in the physical aspects of her safety. She could, after all, take care of herself. He had seen her in action too many times not to feel, in some vaguely Christian sort of way, a small amount of compassion for the enemy.

And such an emotion was rather tricky to handle. It was difficult being on the side of Right all the time, more so when you were compelled to grind the enemy into dust, scatter his ashes to the four winds, and pickle his innards so they might not be resurrected in the future by some unsuspecting fool who'd gotten hold of an ancient formula found in an ancient book discovered in some small dusty shop tucked away in some forgotten corner of some teeming city where the population was too sophisticated to understand how evil bred in its guts, its veins, its decadent moral structure.

He sighed.

He parted the plant again and saw a curious-looking man standing at the desk with a statuesque blonde. He leaned back, suddenly leaned forward and parted the plant again. The blonde! He knew her! She had been at the commotion earlier in the evening! And here she was, a native of this community, taking a room for the evening.

Perplexed, he strained close to bursting his tartan waistcoat to eavesdrop on their conversation, his eyes widening in astonishment when he realized they were speaking of a meeting the next morning. Here! In the lobby!

His mouth opened in amazement as he understood that the participants of this meeting were going . . . Good lord! They were going to confront *him* in his very den! During the safety of the daylight hours!

He gasped as his quicksilver mind rapidly assimilated the heartening yet ominous implications: that he was not the only one who knew the secrets of the Inner Circle, that band of intrepid professors dedicated to the eradication of the supernatural forces that threatened to overwhelm the world; that he was not the only one who had the supreme fortitude to face the One Creature of the Night all men feared, and a handful of women too, those who weren't trying to crawl into *his* bed; that he was not the only one who would willingly defy Death itself in order to rescue mankind from a fate worse than death, even if death was a pretty big part of it.

He was so staggered by the revelation that a sheen of perspiration slipped chillingly across his brow.

How did they know?

Was there a rival group of righteous Evil eradicators of which he had been unaware all these years?

Or had someone in the Inner Circle been tortured to reveal all?

He slumped back in his chair as the woman headed for the staircase, and the man who looked like a seedy pirate stumped off toward the exit; he sighed as the woman disappeared upstairs, and the man with the attached rubber chicken vanished into the night, a puff of fog drifting into the lobby before the door closed behind him; he shook his head in dismay and disbelief as the clerk began the tedious job of taping the rug back together where the man who looked like a seedy pirate's clawed foot had left runs in the threading.

He was crushed.

He was devastated.

As he stroked his immaculate goatee in agitation, he was reminded of the time he and Dianna had dispatched to Hell the insidious Viper of Bendargen, and how there too a handful of brave peasants had happened upon the arcane lore, and had helped him in his victory. They had died. Pretty horribly, in fact. But they had, indeed, helped him.

So maybe it wasn't so bad after all.

He allowed himself a brief smile.

If he were somehow able to become part of this courageous group of local peasants, there was a chance that this, the greatest of his enemies, might be defeated without harm to his own corpulence.

He allowed himself a tiny grin.

And if they died and left him the only survivor, he'd get the Inner Circle reward, not to mention Man of the Year for the sixth year in a row.

He crossed his legs and ran a manicured finger along his club tie.

It would have been seven in a row, though. Should have been seven. He could have had seven without raising a sweat if it hadn't been for some idiot constable in Bavaria who had mistaken him for a vagrant and had thrown him in jail, thus permitting the Sadist of Lillinga to escape his clutches.

But, he thought magnanimously, there's no use crying over spilt ichor.

Had it not been for that officious Bavarian fool, he never would have stumbled across the vital clues which had ultimately led him to the illuminated manuscript which had allowed him access to the ribbon-tied letters which had led him to the address in Canterbury where, in the attic, he had discovered the splintering trunk in whose false lid he had found the yellowed map which had led him to the fallow field outside Nottingham where he had unearthed the disused well at the muddy bottom of which had been the rusted iron box in which he had found the key to the address in Cardiff in whose basement wine cellar he had discovered the bottle in whose cork had been the microfilm which had told him that HE was on his way to North America.

And this, if he was lucky, would get him Man of the Century, not to mention damned rich.

Richer, he reminded himself hastily; he already was rich. He'd just get richer.

He examined the point of his handmade shoe.

It would be difficult. It would be dangerous. It would either be him or *him*, no getting around it.

He looked behind his shoe to the floor, and to the small black ant butting its little head against the ceramic shell-shaped vase holding the rubber tree plant.

High hopes, little lad? he thought with a benevolent smile. In your dreams.

Stiffly he stood, brushed himself off, and decided that a good soak, a glass of wine, and a long night's sleep would refresh him so that tomorrow he would be more than ready to join the battle.

And maybe, just maybe, Dianna would finally consent to give him a discount.

A short laugh, a good night smile to the clerk, and he headed for the staircase, not bothering to turn around when he heard the rubber tree fall over.

Consider it a sign, he told himself, and pray that the little bugger doesn't find the foundation.

• • •

The Reverend Larry Ardlaw stood at his front window, hands clasped loosely behind his burly back. The room was chilly on his bare skin, but he didn't mind the discomfort. He had had a jolly good soul-saving session, and now that the saved soul had departed for her home, which he had learned was in fact a spacious apartment in the stone mansion on the headland since she was, in fact, the Count's housekeeper, he was able to ruminate on all things Good and Holy.

Plus, he was too damn tried to climb the stairs to get to his bed.

Soul-saving, in its way, was as exhausting as sex.

The doorbell rang.

He blinked.

The doorbell rang, insistently.

After a hasty check to be sure his trousers were on, he walked, slightly bowlegged, to the door, opened it, and glared at the two women standing on the porch.

They were not, by any stretch of the imagination, beautiful. "Yes?"

Without preamble, Lavinia Volle said, "Reverend Larry, we got a message for you."

"From the Baron," added Frieda Juleworth significantly as she eyed his bare chest curiously.

"Yes?"

"There's gonna be a meeting in the SurfSide Hotel lobby tomorrow morning," said Lavinia.

Larry frowned. "A prayer meeting?"

"No," Frieda said. "Don't be silly. In the SurfSide?"

"There is no place that God cannot be spoken to," he told them in mild scolding, looked down at his bare chest and saw the scratches. "Damn cat," he muttered for their benefit.

"Right," said Frieda.

"We're gonna go out to the Count's place," Lavinia said, thumping her walking stick on the porch to get his attention back to the matter at hand. "The Baron figures we'll need a man of God, stuff like that."

He almost preened, except that it would have been unbecoming of a cleric in his position, half-naked and all. "And you chose me?"

"Only one I could think of," Frieda said. "Besides, you're on the way home."

"I see."

He wasn't sure how much of a compliment that was, but the women gave him no opportunity to fish. They nodded, left, and left him alone.

He closed the door.

He sat on the bottom stair and took several breaths to be sure he still knew how to do it.

Then he gazed into the disheveled living room and realized with a groan that it would take him all night to put it back together. The hutch alone would take hours to refill, and those throw pillows from the couch were a total loss, no question about it.

But the unpleasant prospect of such manual labor was secondary to the fact that, at last, the good people of Assyria were taking the threat to their lives and souls seriously. He felt his heart quicken; he heard trumpets call on the holy battleground of his mind; he felt the presence of angels hovering over his shoulder. He put his head between his legs and gripped his ankles, breathed deeply, and didn't straighten until the spell had passed. Then he stood, hurried upstairs to his bedroom, and knelt beside the straw cot set beneath the stained glass window on the back wall.

Lord, he prayed, this is Thy Servant, Larry, the Bald One, asking Thee for Thy Divine Help in this most Trying of Times. I have saved a Soul this night, as You already know, but tomorrow will be the most difficult Test Thou hast ever cast in my general direction. I ask therefore that I be Worthy of this Most Holy Challenge, that the steeple get fixed before the bells knock it off, and that the Soul I Saved tonight not be too annoyed in case I have to kill her since she does, after all, belong to a Servant of Evil.

He waited.

Something moved in the straw.

He hammered it to mulch with a pious fist and decided to sleep in the guest room tonight. In a real bed. With real pillows. The cot, for all its dignity and humility, was a drag when he had to think straight the following day.

Besides, he would need all the strength he could muster if he was going to lead the Band of the Good into the Den of the Bad.

"Amen," he whispered.

You got it, a voice answered.

Kent did not spin around in shock or surprise, neither did he utter a small cry of fear at the touch to his person. Instead, he looked over his shoulder, saw the beautiful woman from earlier that evening standing there, and said blandly, "If you're going to sneak up on me, madam, the least you can do is wear clothes that don't rub against your skin so silkily and provocatively. You can hear it for miles, you know."

Dianna Torne sputtered.

"And if you're going to invite me up for a drink, don't bother, because I'm tired, I'm probably going to die tomorrow, and I'd rather do it on a good night's sleep so I can wake up and try to change my mind before it's too late."

Dianna Torne stuttered.

"Besides, the way things have been going tonight, you probably reckon I'm the mysterious Count who's been scaring these people half to death, when I'm actually the Baron, who isn't scary at all. And so, no offense, that lovely designer cross you're trying to poke up my nose isn't going to do anything but make me sneeze." He smiled disarmingly. "And would you mind coming around to the front of me? My neck's getting a cramp."

Hastily, Dianna dropped the cross back into her neckline, stepped around him, and put her hands on her hips, which, he noted, weren't entirely out of oil. "How the hell did you know that?"

"Know what?" he said.

"About the Count."

"I was born a baron," he explained, taking her unresisting arm and leading her into the deserted foggy street. "If I were born a Count, my mother would be twice as pissed, and three times as active."

"Your mother?"

He grinned. "A long story. Would you like a drink? I think Freddie Horton's place is still open."

She nodded. She shook her head. She nodded. She stumbled.

"Are you all right?"

She kicked morosely at a pebble. "How could I have been so wrong?"

"It happens," he explained succinctly. He grinned again. "So you thought I was the bad guy, huh? Whose idea was that, the professor's?"

Her eyes widened. "You know about him too?"

"There are," he said meaningfully, "lots of things I know that people don't know I know because I'm not supposed to know them when I know them. I'm only supposed to know them later, and act surprised when I find out that I really knew them all along." He blinked; he was making himself dizzy. "Anyway, this is a small American town and, just like small towns in my own country, people talk. A lot. To anyone. Especially me."

They reached the opposite curb just as a wolf howled on Nachey Mountain.

"I need a drink," she said weakly.

"I already said that."

She stopped on the sidewalk and looked up at him, which, he noted, made him taller than she. "You know," she said, smiling an admission, "I was actually going to try to seduce you into telling me the names of your minions so we could destroy them after we destroyed you."

He laughed. "Minions?"

She laughed. "Can you believe it?"

He laughed. "Do you really believe me when I tell you I'm the Baron and not the Count."

She stopped laughing. "Son of a bitch."

"Ah, you have met my mother."

Even in the fog, and probably because of the diffused light coming from the MooseRack, he could see a dark look pass over her face.

"You're toying with me, your lordship," she said angrily, "and I don't appreciate it. I made a mistake. A stupid mistake. So I'm sorry, okay? That's an apology. Now, if you'll excuse me, I think I'll return to my room and get some sleep."

Kent, lad, he thought, sometimes you are one great soddin' ass.

He touched her arm as she turned to leave.

She stopped with a disdainful stare.

He said, "Look, Miss . . ."

"Torne."

He touched his jacket. "I know. Roxy did it. Strong woman, that one is. It must be the blowfish."

She couldn't help herself; he could see that and commiserated when she said, "Blowfish?"

He smiled apologetically. "Another story, but not as long as the one about my mother." He tilted his head toward the entrance. "A nightcap, and a truce, what do you say? I'll tell you about the blowfish, you tell me your story, and perhaps, by the time Freddie throws us out, we'll not be so mutually antagonistic at a time when allies are evidently hard to come by."

Doubt tinged her slow acceptance.

He shrugged without moving. If this was indeed the professor's assistant, perhaps he could learn something about killing supernatural beings without being killed himself. And if not, it wouldn't be a total waste of time.

He wasn't sleepy.

He probably wouldn't sleep at all.

Several automobiles sped past, heading south, mattresses and rocking chairs tied to their roofs.

"Zaguar," she whispered.

Quickly he checked the curbs and the street. "No kidding, where? I've always wanted one, you know. Never saw one here before, though."

"You're doing it again," she warned.

"Doing what?"

"Messing with my mind."

Kent reached for the door, pulled his hand back, looked at the street, at her, at the fog, at the rip in his jacket. This, he suspected, was not going to be easy.

"Zaguar," he said, to be sure she had said it first.

She nodded.

He gestured for her to continue.

She sniffed, cleared her throat, and looked at him sideways. "Zaguar."

He smiled. "So far, so good."

"Lamar de la von Zaguar."

He smiled, but it was hard.

"Lamar?"

Her look was unreadable.

He decided to turn the page. "And he is . . . ?"

"The Count."

His eyebrow lifted. "You mean, Count Zaguar? *The* Count Lamar de la von Zaguar?"

"Jesus Christ, you know him?"

His left hand waggled. "I've heard rumors, nothing more."

"Amazing," she said to herself. "But if you know so much, why are you still here? Why haven't you run away to wherever it is you run to when you need to run away?"

He grunted. "I did. That's one of the reasons I'm here."

"Ah."

"Yes."

A dented, gasping, lopsided pickup rattled along the street, backfiring several times before swaying around the corner. As he followed its jerky progress, his gaze happened to catch a portion of the set-back-from-the-street funeral home, and he wondered if the redoubtable Miss Bingham had discovered anything unusual about the victims Dick Walker had brought to her that night. Other, he amended, than the lack of blood, the single mark on the side of the neck, and a potential for having the propensity to leave one's grave at awkward, if not embarrassing, moments.

Dianna tapped him on the chest.

He shook the wondering off as an unhealthy trail to follow for much longer. If he went over there, if he asked, if the undertaker showed him, he'd have to look at a corpse. This was not part of the plan.

Instead, with a grand, almost self-mocking flourish that brought a genuine smile to her lips, he opened the door, followed her in, and in a moment of regrettable forgetfulness yelled, "Good lord, Mother, not again!"

– V –

Interlude With Count And Minions

The ancient stone mansion that had no name had a pretty big dining hall, two fairly large parlors, and a kitchen immense enough to house the Roman Army in the glory days of the year II. There were also rumored to be fourteen bedrooms, several bathrooms, a basement that had tunnels leading to other tunnels that led to the basement, and an attic of such proportions as to make the rest of the house look fairly large. The turrets on the four corners were in a class by themselves, but expected to graduate any day now.

But it was in the library that Count Lamar de la von Zaguar chose to gather his forces for their final meeting. It was an unsurprisingly large room with a walk-in fireplace, several pieces of still serviceable furniture, built-in bookshelves now standing empty, a long Lepeche-polished refectory table at which, in former times, many people sat playing a complex game of cards long since forgotten, and high arched windows covered now with thick, dark velvet drapes.

And here, as in the rest of the mansion, all the mirrors had been taken down and shattered, the pieces scattered off the cliff.

The Count stood at the head of the table, his hands clenched in tight bloodless fists.

"You will be quiet and listen!" he hissed angrily. And immediately shut up because trying to hiss menacingly latcly meant that he also spit and sprayed through the gap left by his collision with both beach boulder and chapel steeple. It was not the image he required or desired for his conquest, and the dentist had told him it would be weeks before the cap would be ready.

He passed a weary hand over his face.

Eight centuries, give or take a turbulent decade, had not given him so much trouble in establishing a beachhead of heinous rampage as had this miserable bunch of fishermen and merchants. In Maine, of all places.

But in a rare moment of self-admitted honesty, he realized that he welcomed it, too; that he welcomed the challenge. Eight centuries also tended to get rather boring when the people you attempted to suborn were so bloody predictable.

"Are you all right?" Belinda Durando asked solicitously.

He nodded.

"Got another contract," offered Jared Graverly proudly, dropping the papers onto the table and beaming. "They insisted on keeping the pink light, though."

He nodded.

Dwight swallowed quickly when he realized he was expected to say something as well. "The food's pretty good."

The Count nodded.

In a shadowy corner of the room, three young women in expensive filmy white nightgowns much too thin for the weather giggled and hissed and generally carried on in a grotesquely coquettish fashion until he glared at them to be silent. They glared back. He smiled at their spunk. He liked living dead with spunk; they kept him on his toes.

Now if only he had someone of a more mature nature to share his destiny with him, a companion, a helpmeet; someone who could love him for what he was inside, not for what he was on the outside even when he was a mysterious sparkling mist or that damn wolf; someone who could overlook his once-human faults and fill the vast emptiness that weighed heavily upon his heart.

It was the reason he had come to America.

To find . . . a wife.

He glanced around the table.

His minions waited expectantly.

"It is," he announced at last, "almost time to begin the end."

Dwight looked at his watch.

"Soon the Assyrian peasants will attempt to storm the castle."

Graverly wiped a bit of grease from his brow and gazed perplexedly around the room.

"And we shall be waiting."

After a short hesitation, they applauded.

He smiled without parting his lips. "As it is now after midnight, I can safely say that tonight will see the destruction of that fat little toad with the pointy beard and all who walk with him against forces he cannot, never had, and never will understand because he is, always was, and always will be a flaming idiot."

They applauded.

Dwight reached for a spider he'd stuck under his chair for gastronomic emergencies.

The Count's voice rose dramatically: "And when we are successful, you shall all be rewarded beyond anything you have ever dreamt of!"

Graverly grinned. The consequences of an immortal real estate agent were too explosive and wonderful to contemplate for long without drooling.

Dwight swallowed, hoping that this wouldn't ruin the completion of his memoirs.

And Belinda Durando couldn't help thinking about the minister she had attempted to sway to their side only a few hours ago.

The Count gathered his cloak about him imperiously. "I shall rest now. Dawn is almost upon us."

He strode to the large oaken door, opened it, paused, looked over his shoulder.

"But if you fail me," he warned, his red eyes staring straight at his housekeeper, "there shall be no escape from de la von Zaguar's eternal wrath!"

He sneered, wiped the spit from his chin, and vanished.

- **VI** -

The Peasants
Mass,
With or Without
An Apostrophe

◆ 1 ◆

There was nothing even remotely auspicious about the following day in Assyria. In Maine. Shortly after dawn, the sky had filled with low scudding clouds pushed off the sea by a steady moaning wind; the temperature had, despite the season, dropped to something more akin to early autumn in Alaska; and the streets were virtually deserted. Not an automobile was to be seen either at the curb or on the road. Shops were open, but there were no customers. A handful of people walked the beach, but no one ventured into the water. The fog had lifted, but there was still a slight dampness to the air.

Kent was not enthusiastic.

Coming to the mansion on the headland during the daylight hours was supposed to signify sun, a delightful onshore breeze, sea gulls wheeling carefree over the surf, and squealing children playing on the sand. It also meant seeing things much more clearly and with a clear head, which should have meant that none of this talk about vampires made any sense at all to a reasonable man.

However, standing at the mansion's formidable front door, the wind beating the hell out of his hair and the surf pounding the hell out of the rocks at the base of the cliff, only served to make it all the more real for reasons he could not understand but was forced to accept if he planned to get out of this alive.

Which he did, in case anybody was wondering.

Behind him, waiting at the foot of the wide stone steps, were the professor and his assistant, the officially uniformed Dick Walker, Roxanne, Reverend Larry, and Captain Tackard, who had put a feathery sweater over Bruno to ward off the chill and evil spirits. The two gravediggers had begged off, explaining that they had a lot of work to do before nightfall, what with Salem and Plimsol and all still being dead. Freddie and Mabel claimed they had a restaurant to run and a daughter to figure out how to kill since the baron wouldn't lift a finger to help them. And the clerk at the hotel had made everyone pay up before he'd let them leave the building.

Kent sighed.

Then he blew loudly in exasperation when the wind took Walker's cap and pinwheeled it across the lawn. Which in itself did not exactly inspire one to suggest a fast game of cutthroat croquet. It was one hundred fan-shaped yards of beaten brown grass and leafless twisted shrubs ending at a low wood railing that wouldn't have stopped a ghost from shrieking over the edge to the turbulent water below. When the chief returned puffing and panting with his prize, Kent took a deep breath and knocked on the door. Again. He had been knocking for nearly ten minutes and so far nothing had happened except that his knuckles stung like the very dickens.

"Try the doorbell," Roxy suggested.

"There isn't one."

"Try the doorknob," the chief suggested.

"It doesn't turn."

"O Lord," cried Reverend Larry, "allow us, Thy Humble Imperfect Warriors, entrance into this suspected Lair of Evil in order that we might do Thy Work before Thy Sun sets yet again and Evil stalks our Humble Land!"

There was no lightning either.

The professor, bedecked in a deerstalker hat and matching Inverness cape, rolled his eyes agnostically at the cleric's well-meaning incantations, puffed up the steps, and placed a small black medical bag on the stoop. "Maybe," he said as he opened it, "I have something in my bag."

"A key?" Kent suggested wryly.

The little man glared.

Kent shrugged. But at least the professor was speaking to him, which was more than he could say for Dianna Torne, who hadn't said a word since the polar bear had attacked him last night, disguised as his mother. In fact, she had left the restaurant instantly, leaving him to have both their nightcaps. When he woke up, stretched out across the bar and covered by a checkered tablecloth, Roxy had been sitting beside him.

"Funny," she said with a totally unsympathetic smile, "you don't look like a baron."

"Funny," he'd growled, "you don't look like Tugboat Annie."

Nevertheless, after scolding him because she'd been hunting all over town for him and it was already past midafternoon, she had fed him a steak, cured his hangover with a hair of the dogfish, and had made sure he hadn't forgotten his vow to lead them all to the mansion that morning. He hadn't, but he'd been hoping she had.

By the time he felt human, it was already nearly four.

By the time he had rapped on the door for the hundredth time, it was just after five o'clock, since it had taken them forever to get up the road so heavily blocked with fallen trees, uprooted shrubs, and a couple of massive boulders.

Thank god, he thought as he raised to his hand to knock again, for daylight-saving time. We still have a couple of hours we dare not waste.

He knocked.

No one answered.

He folded his arms in disgust and leaned back against the jamb. "You know," he said to Tarkingdale, "this might be a good time to tell these nice people why we're here."

The professor looked at him as if he were out of his baronial mind.

"I mean," Kent continued, "he's a vampire and all, but who, exactly, is he?"

Tarkingdale straightened, pinched the bridge of his nose, and admitted that it was probably a good idea. After all, some of these people may not return alive, and it would be nice to know what they had died for.

Kent suggested that the man could probably have chosen a more tactful, more heartening, more optimistic way to put it.

Tarkingdale apologized.

Kent lifted a shoulder in a *that's nice even if it's too late* gesture.

The professor looked at the Assyrian army and said, "His name is Lamar de la von Zaguar."

"We know that already," Kent whispered helpfully.

"Damnit, there he goes again," Dianna complained.

"Aside from the famed Count Dracula of Transylvania infamy," Tarkingdale continued unperturbed, "he is probably the third or fourth most feared and reviled Creature of the Night extant in the world today. It is my studied and irrefutable contention that he is here, in America, to find a mate." He sniffed. "Well, not exactly a mate in the mating sense of the word, you understand, but someone to be his eternal companion, his lover, his friend, his partner in degradation and disgusting supernatural practices." He leaned forward. "He is vicious, my friends, make no mistake about it. He will stop at nothing to achieve his goal. Nothing!"

"But why is he trying to buy up the town?" Roxy asked.

"To provide a refuge for his undead minions," Kent ventured. "Kind of a vampire haven."

Dianna poked the chief's arm. "How the hell does he do that?"

"Exactly," the professor agreed, nodding eagerly. "And once he has established his unearthly domain here, it will only be a matter of time before he has spread his evil seed across the entire continent."

The wind howled mournfully through the stone eaves.

The sea pounded the foot of the cliffs.

"Pretty awful," Walker finally said.

"An Abomination!" agreed Reverend Larry.

Kent waited.

The professor fumbled in his black bag.

"That it?" Kent asked.

"Pretty much," Tarkingdale answered.

Kent said, "Okay," and knocked on the door again.

And again, nothing happened.

The professor pulled a gold-trimmed leather strap from his bag and whacked it against the thick oaken door. Nothing happened.

"O Lord," Larry cried, "let not the Evil One stop us now from Our Divine Purpose."

The professor tried waving a jewel-studded rope over the plugged keyhole. Nothing happened.

Claw fiddled with his concertina until the bow broke.

Kent looked up at the imposing structure, at the huge blocks of weather-stained granite, at the high arched windows coated with grime and salt, and sighed.

The professor took out an exquisite ax made of onyx and cured lead. The blade broke. Nothing happened.

"O Lord," cried Larry, "give us the Strength to find the Way, the Truth, and an open Window!"

"Oh lord," Roxy muttered, "put a sock in it."

The professor closed his bag and shook his head. "It is much stronger than I imagined," he said, defeat in his voice, his goatee trembling in indignation. "*He* is much more powerful than I've been led to believe."

Swell, Kent thought; the expert is stumped.

Roxy looked at the door, examined the huge iron hinges, peered closely at the join between wood and frame, then reared back and kicked it.

The door opened.

She grinned.

Kent looked at her steadily, fearing that if he asked, she would give him an answer that would make him feel like a jerk and want to hit her.

And suddenly they were quiet.

It was time.

To go inside now, to enter the lair, meant that some of them might not ever come out again, alive; to venture across that daunting threshold meant that the battle would commence without mercy to either side; to stand out here in the damp and the cold and the godawful wind would mean half of them would be blown off the cliff unless they went inside to certain, and probably pretty horrible, death.

The professor reopened his little black bag.

Kent said, "In for a penny, lads and lassies," and with a squaring of his shoulders, moved to enter.

"Wait for me," Roxy said. "I have a stake in this too, you know."

"So do I," said the professor. "But I think we should wait until we corner the vampire in his coffin."

"O Lord!" cried Larry.

The concertina rumbled.

But Chief of Police Walker beat them all to it, shoving his way to the front as he polished his chief's badge with one, black-gloved hand. "We'll make this official," he explained when they sort of protested but not very loudly. "If I barge in first, it's constitutional; if you do, it's breaking and entering and I'll be forced by my loyalty to my solemn oath of office to throw you all in jail until you can make bail."

Kent stepped aside immediately.

Roxy glared at him. "Coward," she muttered.

"Deportation," he countered.

And one by one they followed the stalwart Assyrian chief of police and part-time lawyer into the forbidding mansion that had no name.

It was huge.

There were cobwebs swinging and swaying all over the place, and dust lay in thick layers over just about everything, including several human skeletons crumpled against the baseboards.

"Now what?" Kent asked Walker.

They stood in the middle of a vast central hall. Stairs to the second floor were directly ahead, open doorways were to either side, and a short corridor led toward the back; on the walls were brackets that held rather tall, unlit torches.

The chief backed away. "Don't ask me. I got us in here legally. Now it's your turn."

Kent curled a lip.

Walker unsnapped the cover of his holster to expose the butt of his specially made .38 Special.

Tarkingdale extracted a small thick notebook from his coat pocket and leafed quickly through the pages. "I can't find it," he complained to Dianna, waving the book in her face. "Damn, I can't find it."

Impatiently, she took the book from him, turned to the last page, read a few sentences, and said, "It's the wrong one. This is for the Harpy of West Mongolia."

"Which means?" Kent queried.

"In layman's terms," she explained simply, "we ain't got shit to work with."

The professor began searching his other pockets. "Don't be too hasty, my friends. It's got to be here somewhere. I am, always, prepared."

Kent stepped toward the staircase, hands on his hips. This had been a beautiful place in its time, he could see that by the elaborate stonework, the frayed but still magnificent tapestries on the walls, the empty portrait frames coated in gold and silver, the marble pedestals that had once held vases of exquisite design; but its time had passed about a hundred years ago. And if he knew anything about centuries-old mansions, it was this: it would take them weeks to search it thoroughly, and even then, the Count could keep moving his coffin from one place to another and they'd never catch him.

Never.

Ever.

"So where do we start?" Roxy said, joining him, her hands on her hips.

"Bruno might be able to help," Claw said, joining them, his hands on his hips. "Got a good nose for dead things, so to speak."

"How about a prayer?" asked Reverend Larry.

They looked at him.

He put his hands on his hips.

"No," hissed Dianna to Tarkingdale, "that's for the Banshee of Christmas Yet To Come."

Kent came to a decision. "It's dark in here."

They nodded wisely.

"So we'll start by opening some of the drapes in these front rooms so we can see what we're doing. The sun will be gone in a little while. We need more light. It's either that or we carry candles around all day and drop hot wax on our hands."

Pleased to have a task at last, they bustled into the lefthand parlor and threw open the drapes, releasing dust, strips of rotting velvet, and light into the room.

"Let the sun shine in!" Reverend Larry called cheerfully.

After a swift but expert search that revealed nothing but more dust, and some icky rat bones, they hurried into the opposite room, passing the professor and his assistant, who were still huddled in the hall, tossing tiny notebooks onto the floor in disgust.

"We're going to die," the little man moaned.

"Face it with a grin," Reverend Larry counseled them as he patted Tarkingdale on the shoulder.

"Stupid git," Dianna spat.

Kent couldn't help it; he grinned broadly and said, "Now, now, now—smilers never lose, Miss Torne, and frowners never win, don't you know."

"My heavens," the minister said in astonishment. "I didn't know you read the Scriptures."

Kent stared at him.

Reverend Larry whistled a painfully happy tune and skipped into the other room just in time to greet slanting rays of grey light exposed by the creaking collapse of a brass curtain rod over the four front windows. He applauded reverently. "Splendid! Just splendid!"

Two more rooms were similarly enlightened.

Then Roxy found the light switches, all cleverly disguised as ornamental ceramic doorknobs glued to the walls.

The professor stripped off his coat and trembled with indignation as Dianna searched his suit seams and pockets. "I just couldn't have forgotten it."

By the time the main group had reached the kitchen, Kent figured the place was exposed to more light than since the roof had been put on. But still there was nothing, except in the dining room.

"Somebody's eaten here recently," Roxy declared as she pointed to the plates, the goblets, and a couple of tiny hairy hinged legs.

"So where are they?" Kent wanted to know. He thumped a fist against his leg. "God knows we've been making enough noise around here." He had a thought; he hated it. "Good lord, they're not all vampires, are they?"

"Well, Jared certainly isn't," she answered as Reverend Larry and the chief poked through the Sheraton sideboards while Claw sat in an Empire-inspired thronclike chair and fed roach crumbs to Bruno.

"I can't believe it!" the professor yelled.

That tears it, Kent decided, patience gone with no forwarding address. Motioning to the others to follow, he marched back to the center hall and grabbed the professor just before the man took off his underwear. Which, Kent noted with some satisfaction, had colorful pictures of waltzing whales and spinning unicorns all over it. Top and bottom. He looked at Roxy, who grinned, and shrugged.

"What," he demanded, "the hell are you looking for?"

The little man backed away skittishly and took his outer clothing one piece at a time from Dianna's arms as he answered, "The rules, you fool! We cannot even begin to comprehend what we are up against, nor can we fight *him* once we do comprehend, until we have the rules!"

Dianna stuck out her tongue.

A stream of dust filtered down from the ceiling.

Kent watched the dust, and felt an uncanny sensation of being watched himself. They were not alone.

"Count Zaguar is a vampire, yes?" he said.

The professor nodded as he would to a dim student.

"You kill vampires with sunlight, stakes, cutting off their heads and filling the mouth with garlic, and stuff like that, yes?"

The professor stopped working on buttoning his paisley waistcoat.

"We repel him with crosses and garlic and holy water, right?"

Dianna gripped her boss's shoulder tightly.

"He doesn't cast reflections in mirrors, can't travel over running water, and this one probably only has one fang. Right?"

Trembling mightily, the professor nodded as he drew a Belgian garlic cross from under his pink-striped shirt.

"So what the hell are you looking for!" Kent yelled.

The professor waved the cross in front of him. "You . . . you *know*!"

Dianna danced to stay behind him. "He knows a lot," she whispered loudly. "You should hear all he knows."

"Well, Jesus Christ," Kent snapped, "everybody knows all that crap, man. You're supposed to be able to tell us something different!"

Tarkingdale blinked rapidly in confusion, and tugged nervously on his goatee. He sputtered, his lips tried and failed to form words, perspiration slithered down his cheeks. "Who . . . who *are* you?" he demanded hoarsely at long last. "Who *are* you, that you know all the innermost secrets of the cabalistic Inner Circle? Who *are* you, that you have, with one cruel stroke of your damned Scots accent, destroyed a career decades in the making? Who *are* you, that you should lead me into this horrible place and humiliate me in front of my assistant without so much as a by your leave?"

"Kent . . . Montana."

Kent twitched. He looked at Roxy. "I didn't say that. Did you say that?"

Roxy denied it, and so did Claw, the chief, and Reverend Larry.

Slowly, apprehensively, they turned toward the staircase.

Dianna gasped and produced her emerald cross, which she had lifted from the professor only that morning.

Tarkingdale moaned and nibbled on his garlic cross.

Kent looked up and said, "Well, I'll be damned. It's Belinda Durando."

·2·

Rowena Bingham awoke with a start in her suede director's chair in the embalming room. Cursing sleepily at herself for dozing off in the middle of work, she pushed groaning to her feet and, rubbing her bleary eyes with the backs of her hands, staggered over to the stainless-steel table where Buddy Plimsol lay, naked as the day he was born and twice as ugly. She clucked at the pitiful condition he had kept himself in, then checked the watch she had pinned to her bosom. Her eyes widened. It was almost seven. A quick glance at the window told her that the westering sun had already begun its journey below the mountain.

Damn, she thought; I must be getting old, sleeping the day away like that.

Haste had now become a significant priority.

She turned back to Buddy.

His eyes snapped open.

Without batting an eyelid, and with an economy of motion that would have thrilled a man sixty years younger, Rowena picked up a large wooden cross from the floor and whacked him one across the jaw.

Buddy closed his eyes.

She whirled then toward the other table and said with

clenched dentures, "Go ahead, Eddie, make my day."

Eddie Salem didn't move.

She nodded sharply at her command of the situation, then proceeded with the lengthy process that would, in quick time, fill their bloodless veins with the precious non-bodily fluid that would preserve their bodies for at least a couple of days after Lavinia and Frieda planted them in Heaven's Path. When she was finished, she gave Buddy another whack just to be sure, then went upstairs to call the chief and tell him everything was okay. After which she was going back to the MooseRack to finish her party.

She never made it to her office.

In a foreshadowing of dire things to come, a large hand clamped down on her shoulder and, when she turned, cross in quivering hand, Dwight Lepeche grinned humorlessly and said, "Go ahead, you old bat, use it if you dare; but before you do, you gotta ask yourself if you're feeling lucky today."

She was.

She was wrong.

Mabel Horton stood behind the bar, and beside her husband, and together they washed glasses and mugs over and over. There were no customers, either here or over in the restaurant, but they went through the routine anyway. It was a comfort. It gave them something to do while they waited for the baron to kill their daughter, which they figured he would do because he was, even if he was a baron, that kind of guy. The thought soothed their jangled nerves.

"I'm thinking about selling the place," Freddie said, an hour or so after the middle of the afternoon.

"Thank god!" she exclaimed.

He stared at her disbelief. "What? Mabel, you don't like it here?"

"Here? Are you kidding? Here? With all them ugly animal heads all over the walls? It's like visiting your mother, for god's sake."

He grinned. "Darling, you are amazing. I thought you loved it."

She leaned back and looked at him in astonishment. "But I thought you did."

He shook his head.

She shook her head.

He giggled and dropped a glass over the bar, grinned when it shattered on the floor.

Mabel did the same.

In half an hour every glass, shotglass, plate, platter, and bottle were in pieces; in an hour, every stuffed, glassy-eyed, moth-eaten critter head had been tossed gleefully out onto the street; in two hours, the polar bear was naked to his raw hide; in two-and-a-half hours they were out on the beach, barefoot, watching the water turn dark, watching the clouds rip themselves apart to expose the stars hiding behind them, and tossing pebbles at stiff-legged birds racing along the wet apron of sand ahead of the waves.

"This," said Freddie contentedly, "is going to be my life's work from now on."

Mabel hugged him lovingly.

"As God is my witness," he declared with a broad smile, "for as long as I live, I shall leave no tern unstoned."

In the steeple of the Chapel of Charity, the bells began to toll mournfully.

There was no one in the belfry.

The dog did his stuff.

Dwight Lepeche stood in the middle of Beachfront Avenue and dared a car, a truck, a goddamn tank to come along and squash him. When none did, he raised his fists to the sky and laughed. Laughed. Laughed until the tears came, the hiccups convulsed him, the guffaws weakened his knobby woodsman's knees and dropped him to the blacktop.

Tonight he had proven himself worthy of The Master!

Tonight he had shown all of them, including the three weird women in filmy white nightgowns, that he was truly a part of the team, and not just the waterboy. He had singlehandedly removed as many of the still-living citizens of Assyria from potential troublemaking as he had been able to find. That half of them had already fled to other towns, other villages, other hamlets, other cities, made no difference. They were gone, and that's all that mattered. The others . . . well, Rowena Bingham anyway, was safely hogtied to her chair in her office, there to await the pleasure of The Master.

He rolled over and kicked his legs in the air.

He could have had the clerk at the SurfSide Hotel too, but the skinny man had had a baseball bat and what must have been a pit bull snarling and prowling through the rubber-plant jungle that made up half the lobby.

But The Master wouldn't mind.

The Master was kind.

The Master knew that only Dwight had the ability to roam safely through Assyria during the daylight hours, except for Jared and Belinda; only Dwight had the ability to enter homes without being caught, except for Belinda and Jared; and only Dwight, of all the others, knew the secret of the chocolate sauce.

He laughed.

He giggled.

He sat up when he heard laughter and giggling down on the beach.

Quickly he made his way in a woodsman's sneaky crouch across the narrow parkland to the sea wall, cautiously raised his head over the top, and saw the Hortons gamboling in middle-age abandon across the sand. He frowned, dropped out of sight, and began to chew thoughtfully on his nails, which were, he realized sadly, no substitute for a good Japanese beetle.

He had a problem.

Something had to be done before The Master discovered that there were still living people walking around town that weren't dead. He supposed, after due consideration, that he could always find a gun and shoot them, but what if The Master was hungry? Who would give him the meals he needed? So he supposed, after much debate, that he could always find some more rope and overpower them, tie them up, and bring them to the mansion without a name, but what if The Master didn't want any more visitors? So he supposed, in close to hysterical supposition, that he could find the rope, do the overpowering, and leave them here for The Master to fetch at his leisure, unless The Master wanted breakfast in bed.

Shit, he thought; nobody had told him he was going to have to think to gain immortality.

Then, slowly, a diabolical smile parted his lips.

If all went well, he could kill two birds with one stone.

He looked over the wall, and dropped back again.

Okay, so Horton had already done that. No big deal. The plan would still work, and he, Dwight the Woodsman Lepeche, would come out of this dead, living forever, and smelling like a goddamn rose.

He cackled.

He chortled.

He crept off into the gathering shadows while Freddie and Mabel Horton continued their celebration, blissfully unaware that killing their dead daughter would be the least of their troubles this beautiful late summer night.

·3·

She posed at the head of the marble staircase, a large black-and-silver fan in one hand, wearing long white gloves and a black, slit to mid-thigh sequined gown that could only be called, in the most charitable of situations for consenting adults, slinky as all hell. The effect it had on the foes of Count Zaguar was singular:

Kent grinned.

Roxy slapped him on the arm, hard.

Claw Tackard quickly removed his seaman's cap and clutched it to his heaving chest, hard.

Chief Dick Walker took off his cap and clutched it to his barely moving chest, hard.

Dianna grabbed Tarkingdale's arm and whispered loud enough to wake the dead that weren't already walking around somewhere else in the house, "Jesus Christ, Sloan, how the bleedin' hell does he *do* it?"

"Considering the size of those sequins," said the professor with a catch in his voice, "fairly carefully, I would imagine."

She slapped him. Damn hard.

Belinda Durando nodded regally to Kent, who moved away from the panting or glowering pack, and extended his hand. She smiled and began her descent, one step at a time and holding tightly to the broad banister since her hips seemed to be the only things that were able to move with any fluidity.

When she was halfway down, she stopped to catch her breath, and Kent shook his head in amused disbelief. "Belinda, how are you?"

She returned the smile; shaking her head would have knocked her off the heels that were a good nine inches high and chipped gouges in each step. "Baron, it's been a long time."

"How do you know her?" Roxy demanded.

"Oh," said Kent, "Belinda and I go back a long way. Thirty years or so, I should think. Is that right, Belinda?"

"Oh yes," she answered breathily. Another step. "Easily."

Roxy looked at the woman incredulously. "Thirty—"

Tarkingdale thrust his garlic and sapphire cross over Kent's shoulder. "Back, Creature of the Night! Back, I say!"

Kent knocked the hand away contemptuously. "Relax, Professor. She's not one of them," he said without taking his gaze from the woman wobbling elegantly down toward him. "Well, maybe she is one of them, but not one of them, if you know what I mean."

Claw played something spooky and yet nostalgic in parallel harmonies.

Dianna stomped out of the hall, returned and grabbed Kent's shoulder. "Goddamnit Montana, how?"

Kent chuckled and eased her hand from his person. "I'm not sure if the Americans have an equivalent word for it, my dear, but you should certainly recognize her were you to see her in Regent's Park, or St. James Park, of a Sunday afternoon." He paused. "With a pram."

Dianna gasped in culture shock. She looked up at the woman. Looked at Kent. Looked up at the woman. Looked at Kent. Shook her head and tried to look at both of them at the same time, going quite walleyed in the process. "Impossible. No. Sorry. I can't . . . impossible."

"What? What?" Roxy asked. Then her eyes widened. "Jesus, lady, are you his . . . mother?"

Belinda, two-thirds of the way down now and breathing quite strenuously, smiled coyly and shook her head.

Chief Walker tried to wax his mustache without any wax.

Claw switched to something more youthful, yet mature.

Dianna stomped off again, returned again, and threw up her hands. "All right, all right, I give up. Who the 'ell is she?"

"Shall I tell her . . . Nanny?"

There was a moment of vocal pandemonium as six voices were raised in shrill question, protest, and verbal disbelief. The gist of it, in general, was that a woman who looked that good in a disgusting gown like that couldn't possibly have been the nanny of a man who looked that good in worn denim, even if he was a baron. Yet the fondly rapt expression on Kent's face was such that the tirades slowly petered out, and when Belinda Durando finally reached the bottom step, red-faced and using the fan all to hell, he took her hand and bowed over it before grabbing her in a paternal embrace and planting a kiss square upon her forehead.

Then he turned around, an arm still around her waist.

"My mother, you see, hired her," he explained. "Brought her up from London to see to my education when I was about seven or eight. This was after the nuns, of course." He grinned. "The situation didn't last very long, however."

Belinda giggled.

"I first became suspicious when, in teaching me a life-saving course in the pool, she added a bit of challenge."

"It wasn't a very large shark, your lordship," she said modestly.

"Shark?" Claw croaked.

"Begone, you foul female!" Tarkingdale intoned, a silver-spiral notepad clutched in one hand.

To make a long story short, Kent continued as he led them into the dining hall, that being the only place with enough chairs that wouldn't collapse, Belinda Durando had tried several times to see that his mother became the sole heir to the family fortune, estates, winery, and island, which she then intended to sell and get the hell out of Scotland. When he managed each time to thwart her intentions, his nanny was fired, whereupon she traveled south again and became a major decorative star in several costume dramas of the Gothic horror variety. Shortly after that, she disappeared.

"I assume," he concluded from the head of the table, his voice losing some of its good humor, "you joined up with the Count."

"Indeed she did!" a quavering voice cried from the entryway.

Belinda rose with a gasp.

Kent rose with a scowl.

Reverend Larry marched into the room and stood at the foot of the table. "And now she is one of us!"

"The hell," Dianna muttered.

"My lord, Nanny, is this true?" Kent asked, not daring to believe it.

"Call me 'Nanny' again," she said with a stern but affectionate smile, "and I'll show you just how far this damn fan can open."

Reverend Larry hurried around the table to take Belinda by the shoulders, turn her to face his look of concern. "You do recall our soul-saving session, don't you, Miss Durando?"

The fan fluttered between them. "Most assuredly."

"And did it mean nothing to you?"

She said nothing, only bowed her head in either shame or clever ruse.

Kent, his emotions all atwitter over seeing his nanny again and learning that she was part of the evil plot to take over Assyria, then learning that she might in fact have been turned by the ministrations of a chapel minister, didn't know what to think. Until he looked down the length of the table, past the last chair, and into the front room.

The sunlight had faded rapidly, as if a great cloud were drifting over the mansion.

"I think," he began.

"I wish," said Belinda to the reverend, "that you hadn't come with these people."

"But my dear!" Reverend Larry protested. "How could I not join the Christian Army which besieges this foul place?"

"Banish and Vanish!" incanted the professor. "And take your fan with you!"

"You will . . . die," Belinda bemoaned.

"In the Service of my Lord," said Reverend Larry reverentially.

"Me too, Laurence, but I don't think it's the same thing," she replied.

"Uh," Kent said, trying to get Roxy's attention. But she was busily examining his nanny for, he thought, signs of cracks, sags, and other indications that she was really as old as she would have to be to have been his nanny.

Then a distant ghostly giggling distracted him, and he stared sharply into the corner at his right. Nothing was there, however, but shadow and a pedestal upon which squatted a stone toad.

"I cannot protect you if you will not accept my help," Belinda beseeched the pastor.

"But what about the others? What about your former ward, Mr. Montana, the baron?"

Her fan snapped shut. "Bugger the others, Larry. And Montana, which isn't his real name as you well know but only his stage—ha!—name, can take care of himself. The little twit got me fired, remember?"

Dianna dropped a gold notebook into Tarkingdale's hands. "Try the Borneo Bell Beast thing," she advised.

"Say," Kent said, loudly, futilely.

"It's the makeup," Roxy told him from behind her hand. "It's got to be the makeup."

Claw turned to the somewhat bemused police chief and said, "Think maybe you should call for a little order here, sir, don't you?"

"I'm not hungry," the chief said dreamily.

Claw stared at him.

Walker stared at Kent's nanny.

Reverend Larry threw up his hands in agonized despair. "O Lord, tell Thy Servant what to do about this Servant!"

Kent slammed his fist on the table.

Glances were exchanged, looks defined, and gazes slithered in his direction.

He pointed at the front room. "The sun," he said, "is down."

For several seconds there were several silent interpretations of his declaration until, at last, Roxy jumped from her seat and allowed as how, at close to the top of her voice which had once blasted the earphones off a submarine ensign down in New Haven, that they had wasted too much time gabbing, because the vampires were about ready to leave their graves and have an early lunch.

The professor pointed a wand of hawthorn and garlic at Belinda Durando. "We have nothing to worry about. We shall take her hostage."

Another silence, one that passed strong disapproving judgment on Sloan Tarkingdale's thoughtless decision.

"All right," he said huffily, "all right, you think of something better if you can. I, and my assistant, have Evil to fight." He stalked out of the room, returned and grabbed Dianna's arm, and stalked out of the room with her in tow. "When you're in trouble, give a holler. Maybe . . . I say maybe . . . I'll come to your rescue."

Reverend Larry took Belinda Durando by the elbow. "Flee with me," he begged fervently. "Leave this Den of Iniquity and flee with me to the Chapel of Charity. We shall be safe there if the steeple holds up."

She balked.

He pleaded.

She belted his nose with the fan and tottered swiftly out of the room.

After a painfully lovestruck glance at Kent and the others, Reverend Larry dashed after her.

"Disgusting," said Chief Walker. "You think we should go after him?"

Kent didn't know what to think. Again. Three of his once solid army had defected, and he wasn't looking forward to battling the Count with those he had left. But he wasn't about to retreat, either, not with all those eyes staring at him, waiting for instructions in the full knowledge that whatever he decided would probably kill them all.

Damn, he wished he'd stop thinking that way. It was bloody demoralizing.

"We still have time to check some of the second floor," he said. "If we hurry, we can be out of here by nightfall. And actually, Larry's idea of waiting the night out in the Chapel is a pretty good one."

"Then let's get on with it," Claw said. "I reckon an

hour and a half before it's dark."

"Not much time," the chief said nervously.

"Not if we stand around here telling each other there's not much time," Kent answered with a grim smile. "Besides, it already is dark."

"Okay," he said. "It's your funeral."

Kent gave him a withering, wistful look, wishing he wouldn't keep talking like that. It was more than demoralizing; it was damned depressing.

"Actually," said Roxy as they left the room, "we should check the cellar first."

They stopped in the hall.

They looked at her.

She smiled gamely. "That's where the coffin always is, right? In the cellar?"

Kent opened his mouth to argue, changed his mind and closed it again because he realized she was right. The coffin always *was* in the cellar. Unless, of course, the Count realized who he was up against and put the coffin somewhere on the second floor because he knew they'd be hunting for him in the cellar. Of course, if the Count's enemies had any brains at all, they would know full well that the Count knew they were smart and would look on the second floor first, which meant that the Count, who was no fool or he wouldn't have lived so long, would put the coffin in the cellar because he knew they'd be looking for him on the second floor, not being fooled into thinking the coffin was in the cellar. Which it was.

He sagged against the wall.

Roxy patted his arm sympathetically. "You always do that, don't you."

"What?" he asked breathlessly.

"Make yourself dizzy thinking so much."

His smile was weak, but he refrained from belting her because she was, after all, a woman, not to mention one whose muscles had been truly hardened by constant work on the blowfish-cake machine. Besides, the chief would probably object, being a policeman and all.

He nodded.

He took several deep breaths to regain balance and clearness of mind, then led them into the huge kitchen where, by chance during their first run-through, he had spotted the door to the cellar.

He opened it.

It was dark inside.

The chief pulled out his gun, twirled it and his mustache a couple of times, then dropped it, the gun, back into its holster. "We'll need weapons," he said.

"Damn," said Claw, snapping his fingers in disgust at his forgetfulness all the more poignant since he used to be a pirate and made these decisions all the time until his ship sank. "And that little fat guy with the beard has them all."

"Well, surely," said Kent, "we're clever enough to find some sort of substitute." He glanced around the cavernous room. "We'll need a stake, I guess."

Roxy looked in the freezer. "Sorry. Lamb chops."

Walker stalked to a long empty wood table, took hold of its sides, and dumped it over as if it were cardboard. Then he gestured to the pirate and told him to stomp on the legs with his false limb. Tackard did, soon effectively reducing the table's thick props to serviceable, if not terribly neat, stakes large enough to stop the most ravenous living dead who turned himself into a bat. As long as it pierced his heart and not something like his liver.

They each took one.

With a feeling of not unreasonable dread, Kent stood at the open door and looked down into a deep, dark, mysterious stairwell. "We'll need a guard up here," he said at last. "Someone to protect our backs whilst telling the others, should they appear, where we are."

The pirate saluted. "Argh, your man, sir." He thumped his ivory-and-teak leg. "I'd only be in your way anyway."

Kent nodded solemnly and shook the man's hand. "Good lad, Claw, good lad."

"Aye, sir."

Then Kent Montana, realizing that this might be his last day on earth, and wishing to hell he'd grabbed the professor's little black bag, took the first step down into the bowels of the mansion that had no name.

Two minutes later he came back up and said, "Are you coming or what?"

Thirty seconds later, after a pavane of sheepish sidesteps and mutterings, Roxanne Lott and Dick Walker followed Kent down into the bowels of the mansion that had no name.

·4·

"It's bloody dark down here," said Kent Montana.

·5·

The Reverend Larry Ardlaw pursued his saved soul through most of the rooms on the first floor before realizing that she had, somehow, eluded his pursuit and, somehow, had taken the stairs to the second floor. He knew she wasn't outside because, when he tried to go outside and continue his pursuit in the fresh twilight air, the door wouldn't open. No matter how hard he tried, he could not get it to budge. A quick but earnest prayer could not, did not, would not turn the bolt; a kick such as he had studied from Roxanne only served to increase the pain he felt at losing his saved soul; and when, in a fit of secular intuition, he attempted to open the windows, he discovered that centuries of battering by the sea wind had, with centuries of caked salt, effectively glued the things shut.

And when he decided to try the cellar, the Assyrian pirate on guard told him that the baron and company had already gone down, that if the lady in the sequins was there they would have told him, and would he mind not jumping around so much, it was making Bruno nervous.

Reverend Larry acquiesced readily.

The man made him nervous.

It wasn't so much that he could have sworn that the dead vulture had moved of its own accord as it was the claw that had created several attractive, but ominous, trenches in the stone flooring. As if, he thought as he retreated up the hall, Tackard was sharpening it.

Finally, having exhausted himself and all other possibilities, he stood at the foot of the central staircase and looked up.

He could see nothing.

He glanced around and saw a ceramic light switch on the stone wall. He flicked it, and from somewhere high in the stone rafters, lights flared on. They were not very strong, but they served to dispel some of the gloom which had settled over the mansion.

He started up, calling Belinda Durando's name.

There was no answer but a faint, weak echo.

Wings flapped deep in the upper darkness.

As he reached the top landing, he felt, he sensed, he was positive something was behind him. He spun around, cross at the ready, and saw nothing.

Be strong, he counseled his thundering heart; be strong, for she may yet be saved. After all, she was a nanny. She had a shark, true, but she was a nanny.

There was only one door at the upper landing and, after a quick prayer, he stepped through it.

Another light switch illuminated a chandelier so large he thought he had stumbled upon the set of a motion picture depicting the approach of an advanced civilization. And once his vision had cleared itself of the brightness, he gasped.

The second story was but a single, huge, undecorated, unadorned room.

And in its center, on two ebony sawhorses painted bright green with yellow trim, was a coffin. Behind that coffin, on lower walnut sawhorses not quite as elegantly trimmed, were three others.

O Lord, he prayed, let this not be the One Whom I am seeking since I am still seeking the Other One.

He took a single step forward.

Dust rose from beneath his sole.

The step itself echoed.

On the walls were several iron brackets in the shape of funnel baskets. In these baskets were large torches, blazing away so merrily, he wondered why he hadn't noticed them before. He also wondered why they were blazing away when the chandelier was more than adequate in chasing the shadows.

He took another step.

More dust.

More echoes.

And then, from behind him, a voice said, "Larry, you shouldn't be here."

He turned.

Belinda Durando, now wearing a loose but provocative dark green off-the-shoulder dress, stood by a doorway he had not noticed when he turned on the light to notice the coffin and the blazing torches.

"You still have a chance," she said.

"No," he countered in his best sermonizing profundo, "it is you, Belinda, who still have a chance. Just come with me, leave all this behind, and you will know what it is to be able to walk in the sun."

"But I can do that already," she said reasonably.

He smiled. "No, my poor Lost One. I am speaking of the Sun which lights even the Darkest Night."

Something creaked behind him.

Belinda Durando fussed with the ruffles at her bosom. "I cannot, Larry."

Reverend Larry was perplexed. No one, not even the Popper sisters, had been able to resist his soul-saving before. Even after they had been taken by the Count's vicious fang—which could have been worse; at least the man was neat—he was positive that some trace of Good would prevent them from slipping all the way down the road to perdition. But this woman, this vision, this challenge, this incredibly athletic creature standing so demurely before him . . . she was made of sterner stuff.

With an effort, because she was straightened herself within those ruffles, he said, "If you do not come with me now, Belinda, I don't know if I can help you."

Something creaked behind him.

Her answering smile was at once resigned, and feral. "Perhaps," she said, "I don't want to be helped."

"No!" he shouted. "Do not say that!"

A chill wafted across his shoulders.

Somewhere below, either an organ or the concertina began a slow minor progression up the scale.

Belinda Durando sighed. "I suppose there's no chance you would care to join *me*?"

He laughed derisively.

She shrugged uncaringly. "Suit yourself, Larry." She smiled. "At least you're already wearing black."

He whirled around.

He gasped.

The large coffin was as it had been.

But the lids of the other three were raised.

He whirled.

Belinda Durando was gone, without a sound, without a whisper.

He whirled.

The chandelier went out, leaving him in the flickering light of the torches.

He whirled.

He gasped again.

Three women in filmy white nightgowns stood watching him, and blocking his way back to the stairs.

"Wilma," he said when he recognized the first.

"Cornelia!" he exclaimed when he recognized the second.

"Purity!" he sighed when he recognized the third.

He knew, then, that only a miracle was going to get him out of this plight alive.

The three handmaidens of the vampire giggled and moved toward him.

O Lord, he prayed as he backed toward the center of the room, give Thy Servant a Break, okay?

·6·

"Jesus, it's *dark!*"

·7·

Dianna Torne, after standing in the middle of the hall with the professor watching the Reverend Larry race around like a clerical mistake, decided that no one was going to be able to handle this business but herself. As always. Tarkingdale was still rooting through his black bag, trying to find some secret that the others didn't know, and though she felt a modicum of pity for his crumbling career and his godawful choice of clothes, she also felt something strange, something curious, something as close to loathing as she could get without boxing the little fat man's little ears.

Bad enough, she thought as she wandered into the righthand front room, that she had already mistaken a mere baron for a lofty count; bad enough she'd left the security of the Lonely Hearts Club on Regent Street for the tenuous excitement and boredom of the open road in galvanizing pursuit of evil; now she was saddled with a chubby mentor who'd lost his grip, a group of peasants—and one baron—who thought the coffin was in the cellar when everyone knew that the Count would put the coffin on the second floor simply because the others would all go into the cellar where there was undoubtedly some bone-chilling trap, and a somewhat fierce headache because of all the dust and cobwebs that filled this mansion.

Which, for god's sake, didn't even have the dignity of possessing a name.

Dispiritedly, she wandered from the front room into the library.

Not only that, but everybody had split up.

Now what the bloody hell kind of conquest arrangement was that?

If the Baron had been so damn smart, knowing everything that he did which she still couldn't figure out how he knew it, he should have known that splitting up was the last thing the Good Guys should do. Splitting up meant facing the Evil Guys with less than a full complement of whatever it is they had when they'd first arrived, which in this case wasn't much but it was better than nothing.

And as her gaze wandered over the books in the bookcases, she realized she had a perfect case in point.

For there, standing on the raised hearth of a fieldstone fireplace large enough to be a kiln in another, lesser culture, was a tall, handsome, exceedingly aristocratic gentleman in a tuxedo and opera cape.

She didn't need a business card to know who it was.

"Good," the man said, "evening."

His handsome face was pale, but not sickly. His lips were a delicious dark red, and damned sensuous. His eyes were a smoldering ebony with flecks of enticing red. His onyx brows were arched. His black hair was brushed back and elegantly touched at the temples with feathery grey.

She nodded as she backed toward the door, thinking that perhaps a chubby mentor was better than a sexy killer.

He smiled without parting those moist, dark, not too thick and not too thin lips.

Despite herself, she paused, one hand at her throat, fingering the finely forged gold chain from which dangled her emerald cross.

The man cocked his head. "I think your friends are a little lost, don't you?"

A voice deep, sonorous, resonating.

"I believe," he continued with a sly, knowing, confident, arrogant smile, "the proper phrase is . . . alone at last."

There was something about him, some magnetism, some force, some inner strength and confidence that stayed her from running with a scream back to the hall.

She was in danger.

He *was* danger.

He held out a hand as if to take hers.

She shook her head. Magnet or not, he wasn't about to draw her into an web of illicit love and immortal sex. Unless it was the other way around, in which case, considering her current terms of employment, and considering the monstrous diamond signet ring he wore on his right hand, how bad could it be?

He moved away from the hearth to the refectory table, and leaned against it. "Are you afraid?"

It was her turn to smile. "No. Not bloody likely." And she pulled the cross from the confines of her nervously heaving bosom and let it lie against the taut stretch of her dress.

He started, but did not retreat.

Her heart slowed.

She could hear, through the curious amplifying effect of the mansion's acoustics, Tarkingdale muttering darkly to himself. She could also hear Reverend Larry's footsteps above her, on the second floor. Yet in the presence of this man, this creature, it was as if they were alone.

"You are beautiful," he said simply and directly.

She nodded.

"You have . . . how shall I say it? . . . a way about you. A carriage of class, of superior breeding."

She nodded.

"You appear to be . . . how shall I put this? . . . even reasonably intelligent."

She nodded a third time and tapped her left foot impatiently. So far, he hadn't told her anything she didn't already know.

She knew too that she should take advantage of this pause in the rather blatant seduction to call out for help; she should grab those two pewter candlesticks on the table, form a cross with them and, with her own emerald cross, send the creature spinning helplessly to the ground; she should get the hell out and not stop running until she reached Bangor.

But those eyes.

Those lips.

That gap in his teeth.

Gathering his cloak about him, he perched on the table and shook his head. "It seems as if we are at an impasse, Dianna Torne."

Her eyes widened. "How did you know my name?"

An eyebrow arched seductively. "I know a lot, Miss Torne."

"You too?"

A brief, puzzled frown flicked across his face. Then the smile returned. "I have minions, Miss Torne. I cannot travel the world and do what I do when I have to do it unless I have minions."

Of course, she thought; how foolish of me to forget.

An inner gasp—but how could she have forgotten? It was her job not to forget. Good lord, had he—

She took a small step forward.

His head tilted slightly in subtle invitation, and he rose to his full height. "Come to me, Dianna Torne," he commanded softly. "Come to me."

Her eyelids fluttered.

Her lips quivered.

There was nothing in the room but those eyes, those lips, and that voice: "This will sound foolish, Dianna, but in the short time I have known you, though it feels like centuries, I believe I have, with you, fallen in love."

Something inside her denied it with a scream; something else inside her wanted to know how awful could it be; and something else inside her recommended a break while she figured it out, preferably in another room, maybe even another building, like a church.

"Come," he intoned.

Another step.

"Come!" he commanded.

Another step.

Her right hand moved of its own accord and slipped the emerald cross back into her dress.

The echo of a concertina that sounded very much like an organ, now a trumpet, now an organ again.

He grasped her hands lightly and looked deep into her eyes. "Come with me, my dear, and allow me to allow to you rule the world at my immortal side." His smile filled with puckish humor. "You won't have to pay taxes, you know." And he laughed at the incongruity of the language of amour.

She shuddered.

"But you already have so many women," she said, struggling against the power that slowly wrapped itself about her.

"No," he said sadly. "I have minions. And me they do not understand."

Her own smile was skeptical. "And I do?"

"You fight Evil for a living, my dear. Who better to understand my moods, my passions, my . . . needs."

Well, she thought, he's got a point. However, there was still the matter of—

"But I'm so young," she said, "and you're so . . . old."

He laughed. A deep, rich, resounding laugh. "Yes, this, my darling, I've been told." He pulled her close, wrapped his arms around her, gazed deeply and passionately into her eyes. "But why can't we be just as free . . . as . . . as the birds up in the tree? Night owls, of course." He kissed her. "Why can't we, you and I, have our moment in the moon."

She wanted to spit in his face at such a disgusting suggestion, and at the same time, she wanted to rip off her clothes, rip off his clothes, and do whatever it was supernatural Counts in heat did.

"Oh," she sighed.

"Please," he whispered, "stay by me, Dianna. Be my Countess and the world shall be yours."

She whimpered.

She sighed.

Those eyes.

Those lips.

That tooth.

◆8◆

"How the hell can anyone see anything down here, it's so dark!"

"Will you stop saying that?"

"But, Roxanne, it's dark!"

"I can see that."

"How?"

"Good lord, and you people really overthrew a king? On your own?"

"What people?"

"Barons, dukes, guys like that."

"It was a long time ago."

"The sun was out too, I'll bet."

"Very funny. Look, Roxy, we have a job to do and this bickering is getting us nowhere. It's very dangerous down here, we have no idea what we'll find, and by my reckoning, the sun has already set. Maybe even hours ago, since time passes so quickly in a place like this when you don't want it to. Which means that Lamar has already risen from his grave. So do me a favor—just stick close and we'll be all right."

"I don't know. Maybe I should go back upstairs, okay? See if I can get the captain to help me find a flashlight or a torch or something, what do you think? This is stupid. We could fall down a well or something."

"Be my guest, my dear. But how are you going to find the stairs? It's dark."

"Goddamnit, will you please stop saying that?"

"Enough, you two!"

"Yike!"

"That's better. Now, if you'll stop bleating and whining for a minute, I'll just turn on the light switch here that I found while fumbling along the damp stone wall which, by my experience with old Maine houses, is probably an integral part of the original eighteenth-century foundation."

"Thank you, Chief."

"Who said that?"

"I did."

"Who?"

"Me."

"Which one?"

"Good god, can't you tell?"

"How can I? It's dark."

"Turn on the goddamn light, Chief."

"Jesus," said Kent Montana when the lights flared on and his vision adjusted, "will you look at that?"

– VII –

Lamar's Lament,
Or,
I Fall To Pieces

◆ 1 ◆

The cellar was an amazing architectural example of huge pillars holding up a house. They stood in solemn rows, chipped here and there, discolored by moss and dampness, and festooned with cobwebs. The uneven walls weren't much different, and the floor was made of massive slabs of native rock of such varied shades that their overall effect was one of a madman's idea of a pretty keen checkerboard.

But there was nothing else.

Nothing.

Not even, Kent thought as he glanced around, a decent wine rack.

It was clear, especially in the light, that the Count had not placed his coffin filled with native soil down here.

Without further ado, then, although after a time-consuming thorough search of the entire area just in case his eyes deceived them, he led his companions back up into the kitchen, where the captain told him breathlessly that the professor was still mumbling to himself in the central hall, that Reverend Larry hadn't been seen for ages, and the assistant hadn't been seen for longer than that.

"Argh, I'm a bit concerned, sir," he said worriedly.

Kent nodded, hefted the stake he'd forgotten he was carrying, and cast an apprehensive gaze toward the back windows.

The light was gone.

But he knew that already.

What he didn't know, when he checked his watch, was that it was already after midnight. Now how the hell did that happen, he wondered, and wondered no more since it wouldn't do him any good anyway, and would probably only confuse him.

A couple of bulbs had burned out in the kitchen chandelier too, but he reckoned that wasn't as important as the fact that the vampire-killing sun was long gone, and it was already after midnight, which he wished he would stop thinking since it made his flesh crawl, thinking about it. "Perhaps," he said, "we should leave, and come back tomorrow."

The chief of police nodded sagely and with remarkably restrained eagerness. "Ayuh, that might be the best thing, your lordship. Unless we take these creatures by surprise, there's no telling what we'll find now that they're able to get up and about."

Roxy looked at them in disgust.

Kent returned her look with one of pragmatism.

She countered with an accusatory glare.

He riposted with a rational plea for understanding.

She dodged by hurling a charge of effete nobility who had forgotten what it was like to defend the walls of one's home against forces so great that victory would be that much sweeter if they won.

He sighed a bittersweet reminder that victory belongs only to the living; the dead don't give a damn except that they be buried with all their available parts.

She gave him a glittering tear in the corner of one eye.

He accused her with one closed eye of falling back on the helpless woman ploy.

She admitted it with a bold wink.

He grinned.

She grinned.

The chief, who had been interpreting all the facial maneuvers for the pirate, suggested vocally that they stop all this nonsense and get on with it before anyone else was killed and the tic in his cheek became permanent.

"Right," Kent said.

Roxy hugged him mightily.

"The stake," Kent gasped. "Watch the goddamn stake."

She pulled away quickly, gaped at the dent in his denim jacket, and was about to launch into a series of silent but powerful apologies, when, from near the front of the mansion, they heard someone scream.

Kent ran.

And as he did, he couldn't help seeing the young blowfish machine operator's not all that innocent face dance longingly before him, the promise in those often mocking eyes drying his throat; he heard the urgent words she had used to enlist his assistance in this fearsome foolish war against those who would destroy her home; and he understood exactly what she meant. He often felt the same way about his mother.

He ran on, leaping over a fallen splintered chair, veering around a toppled pedestal, hearing her voice urging him onward, once in a while giggling, once in a while winking. He heard a wolf howl; he heard a bat flap; he heard her again, and couldn't help thinking that the only reason he was here was because he had rocks in his head.

He burst then into the corridor and ran alongside the staircase toward the front door. Ahead, he could see the professor sprawled on the floor, legs kicking feebly, a dark pool of what had to be blood gathering beneath his right shoulder. The man groaned when Kent knelt beside him, noting a puncture wound on that same shoulder, visible now because the cloth of his clothes had been violently torn away.

Though pale with fright and loss of the vital red liquid, Tarkingdale managed a quivering smile. "They missed," he said.

Kent told him to remain silent, tore off a length of the man's shirt, and wadded it into a pad which he pressed tightly against the wound.

"They tried to sneak up on me, the vixens," the professor explained haltingly as Roxy and the chief joined them. "But I used the Crucifix of Lower Volta to hold them off. But there were so many of them. So . . . many."

"How many, Professor?" the chief asked in his best official voice.

Tarkingdale held up three fingers.

"Was one of them . . . ?"

"No. He wasn't one of them. They were women. Young women. I believe they were the traditional three handmaidens of the vampire's household."

Roxy gasped. "Purity," she said to Kent. "Wilma and Cornelia too, I'll bet."

Kent nodded grimly as he tied the padding with a length of material torn from the man's coat. "All the more reason why we have to hurry. The closer it gets to dawn, the stronger they'll become before they have to return to their graves. I think." He looked up as Tackard hobbled helpfully into the group. "We can't take him with us," he said to the pirate ruefully. "We'll have to leave him here."

The professor agreed bravely.

"Captain," said Kent, "would you mind standing guard? The professor has more weapons than he knows what to do with, so you'll be all right, I expect."

The pirate saluted.

Bruno burped softly.

Kent's eyes widened, but he said nothing. The vulture was dead, even with a feathery sweater on. Everybody knew that. It must have been only another part of the supernatural happenings that had begun to affect, and infect, his mind as well. Why, he even thought he saw a ghost standing over there by the foot of the stairs.

Roxy screamed.

Kent leapt to his feet, the chief pulled out his gun, and the pirate ran to stand over the fallen academic.

The figure in filmy white drifted toward them.

"Them," Tarkingdale said weakly. "Lord preserve us, it's one of them."

"Do the best I can," Kent muttered.

Roxy frowned. "Cornelia? Is that you?"

"Roxy," Cornelia Popper intoned. "Roxy, come join us. We'll have a ball. Party all night. Moon the guys down at the docks, shit like that."

Closer.

Kent swallowed when he realized there was not-very-dried blood on her chin.

"Roxy." The vampire raised her arms as if to embrace her sister's second-best friend.

Roxy snarled and backed away. "Over my dead body," she vowed.

Cornelia blinked. "How else?"

And Kent, seized by an explosive rage at the wanton random destruction of such a young woman by such an old man, reared back and hurled his long stake at the now hissing and snarling and growling creature. Then he knocked Roxy to one side and ran forward as the stake pierced the chest of the gasping and howling and screaming monster, tripped the vampire with a clever kick to the back of her knee, and rammed the stake deeper into her thoracic cavity as she fell onto her back.

She kicked; she bellowed; she sighed; she died again.

Roxy sobbed back a sob as a look of angelic serenity spread across Cornelia Popper's restored youthful features.

"Professor," Kent said as he pushed himself slowly back to his feet, "can you see to it that this poor thing doesn't bother anyone again?"

The professor nodded grimly. "And may I say, your lordship, nice work?"

Kent shrugged as he took the chief's stake. "Aye, well, a man's a man for a' that, you know."

"Well said."

Then Roxy screamed again, and Kent saw a second ghostly figure descending the staircase. As he shifted to one side, he could tell instantly by the remarkable similarity in features, except for the bloody fangs, that this was the already fallen vampire's sister. Amazingly enough, however, Wilma Popper ignored the mortals arrayed defensively before her; she concentrated instead on the body lying peacefully in the floor at the foot of the woman who had once been her second-best friend, in another life. The vampire howled in dismay, bellowed in rage, laughed in disdain when the chief fired at her several times, finally stood over her sibling and reached out a hand to remove the offending stake and restore her to her rightfully dead position among the living dead.

Kent wasted neither time, emotion, nor sympathy, although there was, in fact, a second of heroic compassion—he gritted his teeth, steeled his stomach which was acting up something fierce, tensed his thighs, and plunged the chief's stake into Wilma's back with such righteous force that it poked out the other side and ruined the nightgown.

Wilma hissed but once in surprise and, perhaps, just a little gratitude. Then she slumped over her sister's body, not incidentally ramming her sister's stake deeper into her sister's heart. Not to mention her own.

A silence stumbled over the mansion.

Roxy shuddered and looked away from the carnage.

Kent cleared his throat, wiped his hands, and looked at the professor.

Tarkingdale, sitting up now with Tackard's assistance, nodded knowingly.

Then Dick Walker said happily, "That's two," and Roxy screamed again.

Above the mansion that had no name, as time passed more quickly than anyone had thought possible, the late evening, or early morning, stars slowly drowned in a boiling sea of clouds that began to gather over the land.

Lightning flashed on the horizon.

The wind grew in the willows.

Thunder muttered like the growling of a giant.

Reverend Larry heard all the screaming and hissing and growling and snarling, and tried not to panic as he cowered atop the large coffin. The three handmaidens of the vampire had done their best to entrap him, envelop him, and entice him into joining their infamous society. But they had not counted on the fact of his general ministerliness, and the cross he had in his hip pocket. Plus, he ran pretty good too. He figured at least a couple of miles dashing around the second-story perimeter before they figured out that they could do better as bats or mist or wolves. Yet, when they tried, they had failed. One managed a puff of smoke he blew away when he sneezed at all the dust he had raised; a second looked a heck of a lot like Mabel Horton's Scottie, which didn't do well in the intimidation department; and the bat just wasn't maneuverable with the nightgown still hanging from its wings.

By that time he'd run out of breath and had scrambled onto the coffin to make his last stand.

He had prayed. He had supplicated. He had slipped a zillion times on the slippery wood. And he had gaped when the vampiric trio had suddenly floated away, out of the room toward the staircase.

He hadn't moved.

He still didn't move.

He sat crosslegged and waited, shuddering when he heard the unmistakable scream of Professor Tarkingdale, followed shortly thereafter by the unmistakable screams of at least two of the vampire handmaidens.

They weren't pretty screams.

They were the screams of the dead dying.

And still he didn't move.

It could be a trick.

They could be standing right outside the door, screaming their diabolical little heads off, just waiting for him to surrender to a feeling of security, then wham! right in the ecclesiastical jugular.

So he hummed a couple of hymns, worked out next year's budget, picked all the lint off his shirt and trousers, polished his shoes, thumped the coffin lid a couple of times to be sure no one was home, then decided that sitting around like this would accomplish nothing, least of all his clerical obligations to the soon-to-be-destroyed home of his choice.

He jumped to the floor.

He adjusted the cross on his breast so that any vampires who saw him would keep their distance.

He practiced whirling around a few times just in case a vampire tried to sneak up on him from the back, and stopped when centrifugal force caused the cross to nearly jab out an eye.

He was ten feet from the door when the door opened and Belinda Durando glided into the room.

"Belinda!" he cried.

She had changed into a more modest three-piece suit sans tie since that would have obscured, he realized when he noted the sartorial omission, the heaving rosy blush of her bosom coyly shadowed by the glistening material of her deep green blouse. Still, it wasn't provocatively slinky like the last outfit. Which gave him hope.

"Belinda," he said earnestly, "you can see that the three hand-maidens of the vampire have failed."

She nodded in apparent but not provable defeat.

"Does that not tell you of the power of soul-saving?"

She nodded again, and the blush rose from her bosom to her neck.

"Does that not," he continued as he took a slow but determined step toward her, "tell you that this life you lead, with this Denizen of the Dark, cannot compare to the Light of Assyria?"

She took a deep breath.

He smiled at her blatant attempt to arouse him in a manner he had long since cast away with other earthly trappings, except for the soul-saving. He held out a steady hand. "Forsake him, Belinda."

Her shoulders began to tremble.

"Leave him."

Her gaze searched his face as her eyes filled with tears.

Reverend Larry swallowed, for he knew what he must say next and knew not if he had the courage to say it, even though he knew that by saying it he would have to forsake a few things himself, like the soul-saving.

"Join . . . *me*, Belinda."

She gasped.

He was close enough to grab one of her hands.

She did not pull away.

Warily, he cautioned himself against trickery, chicanery, and the clever wiles of a canny woman who had once been the murderous nanny of a Scottish baron. With his free hand, then, he indicated the desolate mansion with a grand, encompassing gesture. "Do you really want to live in a place like this for the rest of your life? Do you," he said insistently, "want to be the housekeeper of a place with all this . . . dirt?"

Shocked at his boldness, she looked him full in the face.

"My house is clean, Belinda," he enticed. "A couple of

sandwiches now and again, tidy the study, the rest of the day is yours."

He could see how torn she was, but cautioned himself against yielding to the foolish weaknesses of the foolish heart. "I . . . cannot pay very much, for I am not a wealthy man," he offered humbly. "But you . . . you alone shall have my undying—" He winced. Shit. "You shall have my eternal—" Damn. "I'm pretty loyal."

She put a finger against his lips. "Laurence. Laurence, can't you see that I am . . . Evil?"

"I saved your soul," he reminded her boldly.

She nodded thoughtfully. "The wrath of Lamar Zaguar is long and nasty," she said.

"The wrath of Larry has done pretty good so far."

Her finger trailed down to his chin. "I cannot help you tonight, you know. Not really. Not . . ." A smile parted her moistened red lips. "Outwardly."

His smile answered hers.

Her shy beguiling smile showed him teeth an actress would die for. "And if I . . . it is so tempting, this life the Count offers, but . . . if I slipped, Laurence, would you save my soul yet another time?"

"Several times a day, if I have to."

"Done," she said.

A wolf howled somewhere deep in the mansion.

"But no goddamn dogs."

Thunder rolled over the roof.

Droplets of harsh rain pelted the walls.

Lightning split a boulder at the edge of the cliff.

Dianna twirled neatly out of Zaguar's coldly amorous embrace just as his tooth closed in for the kill. It wasn't that she was coy; it wasn't that she had abruptly changed her mind about accepting the sort of man's awfully tempting offer; it wasn't the constant screaming and snarling and hissing and yowling that echoed with the thunder throughout the mansion and made clear thinking damn near impossible; it wasn't the sudden graveyard chill that had come over the room despite the warming blaze in the fireplace, set by the Count's continental smoldering look; and it wasn't the twang of conscience she experienced when she thought of all that Sloan Tarkingdale had done for her over the years she had accompanied him on his quests.

"What," said the Count, "is the problem, my love?"

She put a fist to her mouth and nibbled on a knuckle. "I seem to remember that one of the conditions of what you are offering is that I have to spend all day sleeping in a coffin. Right?"

Smiling tenderly, he shook his head. "A fable. A myth. A legend. Coffins are good, but any place sealed off from the sunlight will do."

One eye closed in thought as she replaced her first hand with her other hand. "And the dirt?"

He turned, stared at the wall for a while, then looked over his shoulder. "A nice sheet, a little mattress if you have back problems, but the dirt goes on the bottom. You never even have to touch it."

She bit down harder. "Then I can't do it, Lamar!"

"What?" he said angrily. "After all I've—"

"A ship!"

He blinked. "What?"

"I was born on a ship! I have no native soil."

He snarled; he picked up a chair with one hand and tossed it carelessly across the room; he kicked another chair into several large pieces; he leaned on the table and glared angrily at her.

"A . . . ship?" And wiped the spittle from his chin.

She nodded.

An imperious hand was raised for silence as he thought, schemed, debated, tested, pondered, speculated; he thumped the thick table until it shuddered and threatened to split along the carefully chosen grain; he sat down; he stood up; he said, "A ship?" again and wiped the spittle from his chin.

She nodded.

He shrugged. "Well, that's torn it, I guess."

She sobbed at his cruelty.

They stared at each other from one end of the table to the other, gauging each blink of an eye, each breath, each twitch, each subtle alteration of position.

She feared that she had blown it.

A small but insistent voice told her that not dying was hardly blowing it.

But, she thought, I'd be immortal by being dead.

So what happens in a hundred years, when another young thing comes along? What will become of you? A whispered word to a minion, a pinch of garlic in your midnight tea . . . immortal is only immortal when, dead or not, you're not dead.

Oh my god, she thought; oh my god, what have I done?

The Count cleared his throat.

She looked at him without looking directly into those hypnotic red eyes.

He said, "There may still be a way."

"You're lying," she accused flatly.

His eyes narrowed in hurt and anger. "I do not lie to the woman I have come all this way for to help me in the conquest not just of a nation, but of an entire world!"

She could feel the power of him ripple through the air and slap her across the face. She recoiled, recovered, and lifted her chin. "You have a plan?"

He smiled.

She wasn't sure that she liked that smile. Somehow, it lacked a certain *frisson* of sincerity. In fact, she was sure of it. Yet she had to admit that she was tempted. Not by his previous offer, since she had already proven to herself that she had been a fool to fall under his beguiling spell; no, she was curious about his plan.

"All right," she said at last, hoping that if she stalled long enough, one of those idiots screaming and yelling and bellowing out there would think to come in here and rescue her. "All right, Count, I'll bite."

He laughed.

She winced.

"Too easy," he said, and flew at her throat.

·2·

Frieda and Lavinia stood in the MooseRack entrance, appalled at the scene of destruction spread before them.

"Hell of a party," said Lavinia.

"Must've been. Damn, look what they did to the bear!"

Thunder cracked overhead.

They turned and faced the empty street. After a hard day's and night's digging, they were thirsty, they were hungry, and they wondered if anyone was around to give a damn and take their order. It had been, they had admitted sheepishly to each other, damn spooky out there at Heaven's Path, burying both them potential vampires, even with garlic and crosses mixed in with the soil. Some wolf kept howling on the mountain, a wind came up to rattle the trees, and they were positive sure they kept hearing rustling in the bushes. Nevertheless, they had finished without bolting for the safety of their homes, put their tools in the marble shed next to the entrance, and had walked down to Beachfront with every intention of finishing the party they had started the night before, with or without that screwball, Rowena Bingham.

But the town was deserted.

And the storm was building.

And there, Frieda noted with a poke to Lavinia's ribs, was

Dwight Lepeche, trying to balance an elephant gun on the top of the wall.

"He know how to use that thing?" Lavinia wondered.

Frieda didn't know, but she wondered what in the name of blue skies above he was aiming to shoot at.

"Don't have to aim. The general vicinity'll blow it all to shit."

They hurried across the road, silently, and stood behind the giggling, snorting, cackling, smelly woodsman. Their eyes widened. There on the beach, dancing and laughing and having a better time than any two gravediggers Frieda could name, were the Hortons. It didn't take her long to figure out who Dwight was preparing to kill.

She looked at her partner.

Lavinia shrugged.

Frieda scratched the side of her nose, the top of her head, sneered at the rain beginning to fall, and tapped Lepeche on the shoulder.

"Jesus!" the scruffy pudgy woodsman yelled; spun around, spun back to try to catch the elephant gun, and spun around again when Lavinia took hold of his collar and spun him around.

"What the hell are you doing?" she wanted to know.

Freddie and Mabel stopped their dancing.

Dwight giggled and covered his mouth with one hand. "The Master told me to do it," he said in an oddly high-pitched voice.

Lightning sparked a small fire on the mountain.

Lavinia looked at the Hortons, who were now running toward the nearest stairs, then looked at Lepeche. "You were going to kill those nice folks."

He snickered. "The Master will be hungry after. I wasn't going to kill them, but then I decided I would. They were going to be dead anyway. After."

The Hortons puffed and gasped their wheezing way to the others, leaning on each other red-faced and doing their best to be solemn.

Frieda spun Dwight toward her. "After what?"

With a growl, Lavinia turned him sharply toward her. "Who's the Master?"

Frieda altered Dwight's viewing perspective with a fairly

decent slap to his shoulder and said, "After what, you son of an Edsel?"

Freddie demanded to know what was going on. Lavinia, in crisp but colorful terms, showed him the gun now lying on the beach and explained how they'd spotted Lepeche taking aim at him and his wife with the obvious intent of shutting the Dining Salon down permanently.

Freddie's eyes narrowed and spun the woodsman toward him. "What the hell were you trying to kill us for, Dwight?"

"After what?" Frieda wanted to know.

"Freddie, you think maybe he could do Purity for us?" Mabel asked hopefully. "I think the Baron's forgotten."

Dwight snarled ferally and broke free, ran three or four steps and fell on his face, complaining loudly that someone was spinning the world in the opposite direction of where he wanted to go.

Frieda kicked him unmercifully in the thigh. "After what?" she demanded.

Dwight cowered, cringed, sniveled, tried to crawl away and was kicked again, this time at the juncture of his legs and his choir voice.

Mabel hid her eyes.

"Nasty," Lavinia said.

"Won't hurt him none," Frieda explained as she grabbed his collar and yanked him effortlessly to his feet. "He never had any to begin with." She shook the woodsman a few times, then threw him up against the wall. "After . . . *what?*"

Dwight Lepeche, tears streaming down his chubby little cheeks, pointed wordlessly and helplessly at the mansion without a name on the headland.

Freddie's eyes widened in abrupt comprehension. "Damn. They actually went and did it."

"Did what?" asked Mabel, wringing her hands.

The rain increased slightly.

The thunder brought a gust of wind.

Freddie shook his head. "Went after the Count."

"My Master!" Dwight wailed.

Frieda kicked him again.

"No choir's gonna want him now," Lavinia observed.

"We have to do something," Mabel announced firmly.

"What?" Freddie exclaimed. "Are you nuts?"

Mabel set her jaw, put her hands on her hips, and faced into the wind so that her hair blew clear of her suddenly clear eyes. "Those people are risking their lives for us, Frederick Horton," she snapped. "They're facing things so horrible we can't even begin to imagine them, except for Dwight here. Are we going to just stand around and let a baron and a little fat professor fight our battles for us?"

A car pulled up to the curb.

"Are we going to let our town be run by a man who can't even shave in the morning because he can't use a damn mirror?"

A pickup parked behind the car.

"How are we going to be able to face ourselves every day in the morning if we let those good people die without us even trying to help them help us?"

Four station wagons, three vans, several motorcycles, and an ox cart parked across the street.

"Will you be able to sleep, knowing that you were run out of town by a man named . . . Lamar?"

Freddie stared at her in stunned disbelief. Then he heard an excited murmuring in the street, turned, and saw the returned townspeople trying desperately to appear as if they hadn't been eavesdropping. He saw in their determined faces their hopes, their dreams, their fears, their pride in the community they had spent a lifetime building. He saw how thirsty they would be in a few hours and was glad he and Mabel hadn't gone into the storeroom.

Then he looked back at his wife and felt something warm and powerful grow in his chest. "By god, Mabel, you're right," he said. With fists firm at his sides, he faced the crowd. "Get your guns! Some torches! Pitchforks, if you got 'em. We're gonna burn that goddamn evil place down to its eighteenth century goddamn foundation."

They cheered.

They wept.

They applauded.

Mabel spun him around and said, "You mean, we're going up there?"

He nodded sharply.

"Up there? Freddie, are you nuts?"

"Well, what did you mean?"

"Well . . . I was thinking more like calling the army or something."

But there was nothing they could do now to stem the tide of the flowering of declared independence. The crowd had become a mob, and the mob was incensed. They had already begun to pile back into their cars and pickups and vans and the ox cart, and were moving in a steady, vengeful procession toward the storm-racked headland. Before Dwight could move to escape and warn his Master, several broke away and grabbed him roughly, trussed him up with some spare netting, and threw him unceremoniously into the back of a milk truck. Another group swept Freddie onto their shoulders, handed him a blazing torch, and brought him swiftly to the head of the line, setting him into the empty bed of a bright yellow pickup.

The mob cheered wildly.

Tearfully, Mabel waved a handkerchief as she receded into the wind-blown distance.

The mob cheered hysterically.

Then Freddie turned around and leaned against the pickup's cab, peering into the dark, listening to the growls and mutterings and cursings of the people who had chosen him as their leader. He recalled his wife's stirring words. He remembered the looks on the faces of the Assyrians. He dug deep into his heart and rooted around for a little courage and some guts.

Then he raised his torch and shouted.

Horns blew.

Speed was attained.

And he knew that by morning Assyria, in Maine, would never be the same.

·3·

Kent Montana had had just about enough of ridding the world of its most recent scourge of vampires. He hadn't realized how bloody it would be, or how noisy they were when they died, not to mention the filmy nightgowns which made the whole thing damned indecent. As it was now, Wilma, Cornelia, and Purity were all in an untidy heap at his feet, each impaled upon the stake of the other in such a complicated fashion that he suspected they would all have to be buried in the same grave. And a pretty deep one at that.

The professor, though groggy, had managed to make it to a wing chair Captain Tackard had hustled in from another room; Dick Walker was reloading his absolutely useless revolver; Roxy was sucking on a lozenge she'd found in her jeans pocket; and there, coming down the stairs arm in arm, blithe as you please, were his nanny and the Reverend Larry.

Life, he thought as he watched the beaming but apprehensive couple, never is what you thought it was when you got up in the morning.

Amazing.

"She's going to be my housekeeper," the minister announced proudly when they had reached the others.

Belinda Durando grinned.

"You have a pool?" Kent asked.

"No."

"Wonderful," he said, kissed his nanny on the forehead, and shook Reverend Larry's hand. Then he flinched when a particularly loud explosion of thunder barreled through the mansion. A glance at his watch told him in no uncertain terms that his ass would be immortal in just a few minutes if he didn't get a move on.

What he needed, then, was a plan.

Tarkingdale pulled his black bag into his lap. "I think I have something here, somewhere, if I can find it, that might help you."

"What?"

"I'm not sure."

Kent nodded.

"I think we ought to burn the place down," Roxy suggested. "That way we get rid of this eyesore and the Count at the same time."

"It's made of stone," he told her.

"Give me a minute," she said. "I'll think of something."

"O Lord," said Reverend Larry.

Kent looked at him.

The cleric grinned. "Not you. The other one." And he looked skyward.

Simple mistake, Kent thought; anyone could make it, no big deal.

"O Lord," Larry continued, "help Us Thy Confused but Righteously Determined Servants in our hour of need and our Search for a way to rid Thy Earthly Imperfect Kingdom of its Evil Living Dead. We humbly ask that Thy Help, however, not be too long in coming since We, Thy Miserable Servants, aren't really Prepared for any of this. And how about some Help on Thy Glorious Steeple, while You're at it."

"Amen," Belinda Durando murmured. And shuddered.

Nothing happened.

"Next?" Kent said.

No one said a word.

I knew it, he thought dismally; I knew it. Give some people a chance to show their mettle, and their iron is rusty. So why the hell is it always me, anyway? Isn't it bad enough I have to spend half my life trying to find a decent part that isn't an English butler, and the other half looking over my shoulder for my greedy mother? Do I have to put up with all this too? Do I have to be the one to do all the thinking, the planning, the execution, the saving? I mean, good lord, can't we just once have a wee *deus ex machina* so that I don't have to worry about dying? Does it *always* have to be me?

Roxy stood in front of him then, slipped her arms around his waist, gazed into his tortured eyes, and said, huskily, "Yes."

"Right," he answered. "I just like to get these things clear, you understand. No sense endangering myself if I don't have to. Continuation of the line and all that."

She nodded her understanding.

"But I suppose I have to."

She nodded again.

He sighed.

She snuggled against his chest for an all-too-brief second, then pulled away, rubbed her hands together briskly, and said, "So. What's the plan?"

Damned if he knew.

Thunder.

Lightning.

Wind.

Rain.

Dust sifting down from the ceiling.

The lights brightened for a moment, then went out.

Somebody yelled.

Somebody yiked.

There were strange sounds in the background, sounds Kent knew were never made when the lights were on because then whatever was making them would be visible and therefore not all that strange, unless the things themselves were strange, which, considering the circumstances, wasn't all that unlikely.

The sounds stopped.

The lights came back on.

Kent, with a forbidding sense of foreboding, cast his attention to the brave but somewhat bemused chief, to the loving couple one of whom used to be his nanny for god's sake, at the wounded professor, to the claw-foot pirate, to the corpses of the corpses, and decided that there was only one thing left to do. He didn't want to do it. He knew he didn't want to do it. But they made him do it.

He sneezed.

That wasn't it, but it was enough to break the tension which had been building since all the lightning and thunder and wind had filled the gaps in their conversational silence.

He thought again.

He checked his army again.

And finally, with not nearly as much reluctance as he felt, he said, "Out."

They stared.

"You heard me. Out." He pointed to the door. "All of you get out. Now."

They protested. They pleaded. They headed for the door while protesting and pleading.

"Why?" Roxy wanted to know.

"Look at them," Kent said, not unkindly but with morbid resignation. "If they don't get in the way, they're going to end up like your second-best friend there, and her sister. The Count is too powerful. Sooner or later, then, they'll be like him and I'll have to fight them all, and I'd rather just have to fight one of those things, thank you very much."

The door opened.

The storm came in, looked around, liked what it saw, and proceeded to wreck the place with howling abandon.

Dick Walker, one hand firmly on his gold-braided cap, shook Kent's hand warmly with the other, probably because of the glove. "You're a fool, you know, Kent," he said with a grim smile and a twinkle of admiration.

Kent shrugged.

The man walked into the night without looking back.

Reverend Larry shook his hand. "I'll be praying for you, you royal idiot."

Belinda Durando took light hold of his chin, pulled him down, kissed his forehead, and said, "Thank heavens you never ate the Yorkshire pudding."

Kent shrugged.

They walked into the night without looking back.

The professor handed him the black bag. "It's in there somewhere."

And walked into the night.

Claw Tackard cleared his throat gruffly and played a timid note on the concertina. "Bruno says to try to make it until dawn." Then he shook Kent's hand.

And walked into the night.

Roxy closed the door, leaned against it, and said, "So now what?"

"Now," he said firmly, "it's your turn to walk into the night without looking back."

She shook her head defiantly. "You kidding? Out there? In all that? Hell, I'll get blown off the cliff. Besides, you're going to need someone to help you." She grinned. "I'm plucky, remember?"

The wind pounded at the door.

The lights in the enormous chandelier, and a couple of the smaller ones, flickered again, alarmingly.

Prudence suggested rather strongly, if not deafeningly, that Kent toss Roxanne out, but there was no time left to argue with a stubborn plucky woman who hoisted sails and anchors for a living. Instead, he hurried to the wall, took down two tall torches from their ornate brackets, handed one to her, and lit them with his lighter.

The lights died.

The wind died.

The rain stopped.

There was still, however, a whole bunch of thunder and lightning.

The flames from the torches cast bizarre, meaningless shadows on the floor and walls.

She took hold of his arm. "Kent," she said.

With one of his patented rueful smiles he shook his head in melancholy refusal. This was not the time. Another time might be the time before their time was up, but this wasn't that time, not this time.

She touched the pocket where the lighter was. "Why didn't you use that downstairs, in the cellar, when we couldn't see and nearly killed ourselves walking around in the dark?"

"I forgot about it."

Her face was a shadowy mask of conflicting emotions. "You forgot about it."

"It happens, Roxanne. People do forget. They do crazy things. They think crazy things. In times of stress they act upon animal instinct, which isn't always rational or very comprehensible."

"You forgot about it."

"Forget it," he told her. "We have work to do."

The plan, such as it was as he explained it to her whilst instantaneously formulating it, was simple: they knew the cellar wasn't where the Count was. They knew the second floor wasn't where the Count was either. Which meant, if they were right, that he was on the first floor, their floor, and it was up to them to find him. What happened next would depend on whether or not the Count was a reasonable man who knew that he faced certain annihilation if he didn't give up his own plan of Assyrian conquest; and if he was a reasonable man, he would quit this mansion and go somewhere else and be someone else's problem. If he wasn't reasonable, however, they would have to destroy him. All things being equal, and with a little luck, it would be dawn by then and he'd be in his coffin and in no position to fight back, assuming they could find it. If he wasn't, they'd have to think of something else.

"Well, hell," Roxy said sourly, "I knew all that already, for crying out loud. What I want to know is, what are we going to do when we find him?"

"Perhaps," a deep voice said behind them, "you'll die."

The bloodthirsty mob reached the end of the road up to the headland.

Freddie saw that the fallen trees and other natural matter cluttering the way would not permit them to use the vehicles with any assurance of safety or speed. He climbed down from the pickup, held his torch up high, and led the way.

Into the night.

Chief of Police Dick Walker stood at the end of the road leading down to the marina and shook his head in self-recrimination.

"This isn't right," he said to no one in particular, even though they all listened because there was no one else around. "We shouldn't be leaving him in there, all by himself."

"He has Roxy," the professor reminded him.

"Like I said."

"Well," said Reverend Larry, "I don't think it would be very wise to—"

Suddenly Belinda Durando pointed. "There! Down there! I see torches and a mob down there!"

Dick Walker felt a bubble of pride swell in his breast and a tear of gratitude force its way into one eye. "Damn," he said pridefully. "Damn."

"Argh, it makes a body feel like singing," said the pirate, unslinging his concertina.

"No," contradicted the chief slyly. "It makes a body feel like having a bonfire."

They laughed, they applauded, they turned back to the mansion and watched in dismay as all the lights went out.

Walker reached then to his holster to get his gun in order to fire a shot to alert the townspeople that he and his friends were up here.

The holster was empty.

"Oh . . . damn."

This really isn't working out, Kent thought; I mean, this really isn't working.

Roxy stood close to him, he stood closer to her, and they both stood about ten feet away from a bedraggled and obviously unhinged Jared Graverly, who stood in the middle of the central hall, grinning maniacally as he aimed Chief of Police Dick Walker's .38 Special at their hearts. One at a time.

"Thought you could get away with it, didn't you," the real estate agent said, giggling and sniffling. "Thought you could ruin the best chance I've ever had to make a fortune and live like a king, didn't you." He hiccupped. "Thought you could find a way to kill the immortal Count, didn't you, before he killed you first."

"It had crossed my mind," said Kent, keeping his voice even, even though his stomach had begun to act up again.

Graverly laughed insanely.

Roxy took a step forward.

Without blinking an eye, Graverly swung the gun in her direction. "No tricks!" he warned. "I'll kill you where you stand!"

She ripped open her shirt.

Graverly gaped.

Immediately, Kent flung his torch at the man's gun hand, knocked the stolen weapon free, and inadvertently, though not unexpectedly, set the smarmy man's greasy hair afire. He screamed, hopped around a little, then ran shrieking out into the night, slamming the door behind him. Kent turned, picked up the torch and the gun, and watched as Roxy rebuttoned her shirt with what buttons she had left, which weren't many, and were very distracting.

When she saw him watching, she raised a shoulder. "Wouldn't have been the same if you'd done it."

He was forced to agree.

"Besides," she added as they made their cautious way down the corridor beside the staircase leading up to the second floor where the Count wasn't, "we could have been there for the rest of the night, you know what I mean? He would bluster and threaten, we would pass a plan back and forth with our eyes, he would be suspicious, we would have to do something pretty desperate, he would probably shoot one of us, wounding one of us badly, and then we'd have to kill him, take care of the wound and go find the Count with one of us bleeding half to death."

"Which one?" he asked without thinking.

She stared.

He looked into the dining hall and shook his head.

They searched the kitchen from cupboard to freezer to sink to pantry.

She opened the cellar door, thrust in the torch, looked around, and shook her head.

They looked behind each drape on every window they could find, and Kent noted that the sky was beginning to lighten over the ocean.

They kicked at walls, at heavy pieces of furniture that looked as if they might have a secret room hidden behind them, at each other when the other one missed and grazed an innocent ankle instead.

Kent began to worry.

Roxy began to look frazzled.

Then, at last and inevitably, they stood in front of the library door, knowing that this was the last place to search. If the Count wasn't here, they would be lost. He would have won, would come back that night, and make sure that they all died a slow and horrible death.

Kent sniffed. "Do you smell smoke?"

Roxy looked around in a confusion that immediately veered toward panic. "My god, I think the mansion is on fire."

"Maybe it's just Jared."

She shook her head and pointed at the ceiling, at the slow curls of smoke gathering up there.

"Shit," he said. "There must be a mob outside, trying to burn the place down and destroy the vampire."

"Now that's a hell of an idea," Roxy said admiringly. "You want to leave now?"

"Yes," he said, and laughed silently at the look of dismay on her face. "But I won't, Roxanne, don't worry. The Count isn't the Count for nothing, you know. He has obviously survived centuries of devious and overt attacks, assaults, and assassination attempts. A few Assyrian fishermen aren't going to defeat him so easily."

"So now what?" she replied, staring nervously at the door beyond which lay her darkest nightmares.

So now, he thought, I'm going to be a complete and utter idiot.

He handed her his torch.

He took hold of the doorknob.

"Be a shame if it's locked," she said, not sounding the least bit upset as she backed away to give him room.

It wasn't.

The knob turned.

Kent took several deep breaths.

The smoke thickened.

Somewhere toward the front of the mansion came the thunderous sound of the front doors being smashed in with axes and pitchforks and a brass shovel blessed by Reverend Larry.

"You could wait, you know," Roxy said, her voice pleading.

"I could," he agreed. "I cannot."

"But why?" she cried. "Why, Kent, why?"

He looked at her over his shoulder. "Because," he said.

She blew him a kiss, and a button fell off.

On the other hand, he thought.

The door flew open.

And something shrieked in his face.

·4·

"You," Dianna Torne shrieked enraged in his face, "are supposed to know this shit, damnit!"

"I—"

"You knew everything else," she screamed. "So how the hell come you didn't know I was trapped in the library with the Count ready to die at any moment?"

Flustered, and a little confused, Kent could nothing more than shake his head.

Dianna raised a hand to slap his peerage into the middle of next week, changed her mind and stormed toward Roxy. "And you!" she screamed. "If you're his goddamned sidekick, why the hell didn't *you* know it?"

Roxy smacked her with the butt end of the torch.

Dianna moaned and stumbled away, screamed again when a mysterious figure stepped out of the thickening smoke and grabbed her around the waist. She slapped at it, kicked at it, finally collapsed against it and buried her face in Professor Sloan Tarkingdale's welcoming shoulder.

Roxy cheered.

Kent stepped into the library and slammed the door behind him.

This, he thought, is it.

And it was.

The library.

Bookshelves, a merrily dancing fire in the biggest fireplace he'd ever seen, an impressively large refectory table with a pair of pewter candlesticks on it, velvet drapes covering a high arched window, pale spots on the walls where paintings once hung, a bare stone floor . . .

and *him*.

He stood regally at the foot of the table, elegant black cloak around his shoulders, tailored evening clothes not at all out of date, a massive diamond signet ring on his finger. And very, very tall.

"So," said Count Lamar de la von Zaguar.

"So," said Baron Kent Montana.

"It appears," said the Count civilly, "that you feel that you have me trapped, is that not so?" He laughed quickly and mirthlessly.

"Not really," answered the Baron politely, who had tried and failed to find another door he could duck through and let the folks outside the door at his back do all the dirty work, because this place hadn't been cleaned in ages. "But I don't think you're going to get away, for all that."

"Ah." The Count smiled cruelly.

Kent moved to the head of the table and let his mind race through the probabilities of killing the vampire before the burning roof fell on both their heads. When plural rapidly became singular, and even that vanished even before he'd caught a glimpse of it, he considered the chances of getting out of here with his anatomy intact.

That he stopped before it got started; he was depressed enough as it was.

"You will die, you know," promised the Count.

Kent felt a spark of anger.

"In fact," the in a sense noble vampire continued remorselessly, "after you die, I think I will take that little fisherwoman who nearly took off my nose, and make her my Countess For Life. I was going to use Miss Torne, but she proved . . . unacceptable."

The anger grew.

The Count moved sinuously around the end of the table. "You see, my dear Baron, you really don't know what you're up against here. You have no idea of the forces you face. This isn't one of your pitiful, meaningless, useless, time-wasting, overblown, melodramatic soap operas. This, you pathetic excuse for a human being, is real life!"

Thunder.

The Count's eyes blazed redly. "So stop this futile nonsense now, my good little man, and let us both leave here alive." Those eyes narrowed. "For if you persist, you little twit, I shall personally see to it that your head is removed from your shoulders. Cell. By. Cell." His lips parted. "And you will not be unconscious during the process."

More thunder.

A raucous pounding on the door.

The Count cast an eye to the door, and the Baron did his best not to gasp when he heard the heavy bolt turn over, locking them in.

The Count laughed.

Kent moved around the end of the table.

"You butlers are such idiots," the Count sneered. "Madam this, and Madam that, and Madam may I wipe your chin, you've dribbled."

"Oh, that does it," Kent snarled, and slugged the vampire square on the jaw.

Zaguar rocked back several steps in shock, surprise, and from the sheer force of the blow. Then his eyes widened, and the red deepened, and swirls of mesmerizing pinwheels appeared in their midst.

"Now listen to me, Baron," the Count intoned in an hypnotic voice. "Listen to your Master, your only Master, and walk into the fire."

Kent blinked.

"Listen!"

Kent tried desperately to look away, to break the spell weaving over him, but the extraordinary supernatural power of the vampire held him fairly strongly, and he was helpless to resist when his legs began to take him inexorably to the hearth, and the conflagration it promised.

The flames crackled.

Sparks flew cheerfully into the chimney.

The Count laughed. "Into the fire, Baron. Into the fire. Where you shall know what Hell is like!"

Sweat poured saltily from Kent's fiercely furrowed brow. His muscles were in agony, and close to cramping as he labored to regain even partial control of his body. But it was as if he were struggling against an animate mountain, trying to walk upright in a hurricane, fighting an army with only a mint toothpick for a weapon. It was no use. The Count had most of him firmly and relentlessly in his hideous thrall.

"In!"

Kent moaned a vain protest as he stepped stiff-legged onto the raised hearth; he tossed his head and groaned a serious objection when he felt the scorching heat of the flames against his skin; he bellowed his passionate rage silently when he heard the Count laughing his triumph.

"In!" Zaguar commanded hoarsely. "In!" Then, much closer, and in a harsh spitting whisper, "Into the fire, you disgusting English dog."

Kent froze.

The Count was confused.

"English?" Kent managed to say, although he did choke a bit. "Did you say English?"

"What the hell," the Count said, "difference does it make? English, Irish, Scots, Welsh, you're all puny and talk funny when you're drunk."

But Kent's anger had already weakened one link of the hypnotic chain, and he called upon the warrior spirits of his departed Highland ancestors, those who had struggled for independence against that very country with which the Count, in his Continental ignorance, had affiliated him.

"Damn you, get burned!" the Count ordered desperately.

But with the last bit of strength left in his baronial body, and with an uplifting image of all those courageous people out there mustering in his support even if they were burning the mansion down around him, Kent yelled a violently explicit Gaelic obscenity to snap that mystical chain, then whirled and threw himself at the vampire.

They met, clinched, and struggled wildly across the floor, punching, biting, kicking, grunting.

The Count put a massive hand around Kent's throat and began to squeeze.

Kent managed to slip his own hand under the Count's strangling hand and slowly began to force it away. His lungs demanded air. Sweat continued to ripple and flow from his flushed brow. He lashed out with a foot and caught the Count on a vulnerable ankle, toppling them both heavily to the stone floor, where Kent scurried about to kneel on the vampire's chest and pound the hell out of it until he realized that this wasn't going to do a damn thing.

He scrambled to his feet.

The Count slowly, ever so slowly, regained his feet.

Kent looked around wildly.

The Count laughed. "Look all you want, mouse, but you'll find no hole to hide in here."

Kent picked up a chair and threw it; the Count batted it aside with a disdainful hand.

Kent threw another chair, then raced to the fireplace and plucked a flaming brand from the andirons; the Count curled his lips, gazed powerfully at the brand, and within seconds the fire was extinguished.

The Count took three swift and long strides toward him, flicked out a hand, and sent Kent flying across the room; Kent landed against the wall, stunned until he shook his head, and stood up proudly.

The Count took five strides toward him, flicked out another hand, and sent Kent flying back onto the refectory table, sliding across it to the far end before he stopped; Kent rolled to his knees and spit blood to the floor.

The pounding on the door faded as the fire ate its way through the mansion.

The vampire threw a chair; the Baron ducked, though a leg caught him smartly on the spine.

The Baron feinted toward the door; the vampire leapt gracefully to intercept.

Kent feinted in the opposite direction; so did Zaguar.

Then, realizing that the time had come for him to make his

final move or die in the attempt, and remembering the sage and prophetic advice of the elderly gentleman in the bar, Kent rose to his full height and looked down upon his enemy.

His enemy looked back up.

Kent smiled.

The vampire sneered, snarled, hissed, and spat.

Kent waited.

The vampire widened his red eyes and prepared to cast yet another powerful entrapping spell.

Kent waited.

The vampire glanced at the door which seemed, oddly, to be bending inward under the blows of whoever remained in the outer room.

And Kent sprinted along the table.

"No," de la von Zaguar screamed when he realized, too late, what was happening.

Kent leapt.

"No!" the Count bellowed.

Kent landed on the drapes.

"No!" the vampire howled.

While Kent pulled down the dark, rotting, velvet cloth and let in the morning sunlight.

The vampire, caught in the destructive rays of pure daylight, threw up his hands to protect himself, but Kent leapt from the table, grabbed up the candlesticks, and slapped them together in the form of a cross.

Zaguar fell to the floor.

Trembling with exertion, Kent held the candlesticks before him, their combined symbolic shadow pinning the unnatural beast to the stone while the sun did its godly work—the skin smoked, melted, dried, peeled away to grey dust; the evening clothes bulged and sagged and collapsed into grey dust; the black Wellingtons spewed more dust as the last of the vampire returned to his earthly origins.

Sonofabitch, Kent thought; it worked.

He sagged against the table and threw the candlesticks aside while a cool draft blew the dust across the floor.

Then the door exploded inward and Roxy threw herself into his weary arms. "You . . . he . . . I . . ."

"If," he said with a content but tired smile, "you're trying to find out if he's dead and I'm all right, the answer is yes."

She kissed him.

He wondered if there were any more vampires around.

The ceiling collapsed in flaming patches, cutting off their escape, filling the room almost instantly with smoke and fire and flying debris.

Without further thought, he picked Roxy up and looked toward the window.

"Jesus," she yelled when she realized what he planned. "Put me down! We'll get killed!"

"I don't think so," he said confidently. "If stone can burn, then there damn well better be an ox cart down there filled with straw to break our fall."

"And what if there isn't?"

He smiled. "What the hell."

And thought again, *what the hell,* as he flung them both through the pane into the free morning air.

- VIII -

Stuff While The
End Credits
Roll

◆ 1 ◆

Sitting on the sea wall and watching the tide come in was not the most exciting thing Kent had ever done in his life, but he reckoned that it was a hell of a lot better than jumping through a window and landing on an ox cart filled with straw. The jumping part was all right, and the straw had done its work admirably, but when Roxy landed atop him, she had managed, somehow, to sprain his right ankle, wrench his left shoulder, and give him a bruise on the small of his back that rivaled the topographical map of Venus.

Still, he thought, he was alive.

Out of work. Out of prospects. But alive.

Roxy sat beside him. Unhurt, and unbruised. She pointed toward the smoking ruins of the mansion without a name on the headland. "Guess we showed him, didn't we."

"Aye, we did that, Roxanne. We did that."

"So now what are you going to do?"

"Don't know. About this time I get some kind of message about my next film, but—"

"Wow," she said, wide-eyed. "Are you into that channeling stuff? Y'know, I have a theory—"

A concertina on the beach played a sprightly march while Claw Tackard played fetch with Bruno.

"You know," Kent said, "I would have sworn that bird was dead."

"It's not a bird, it's a rubber chicken."

Kent looked at the pirate, at the scrambling, stumbling Bruno, and decided not to ask. This was, after all, Assyria. In Maine.

Footsteps behind him tensed his back for a moment until he remembered that the sun was out, the creatures were dead, and the three young women in the filmy nightgowns had been buried without delay. There was, then, nothing to fear.

He crossed his fingers, then yelped when a hand rapped them sharply.

"You'll get swollen knuckles if you keep doing that," said Belinda Durando kindly.

"Yes, Nanny," he muttered.

"We've come to invite you to the celebration at the Chapel," said Reverend Larry. He pulled his straw hat lower over his brow. "Seems there was a check waiting for me at the rectory this morning. Just enough to pay for a new steeple, and a new set of bells." He beamed. "Imagine that."

Kent watched the tide. "Aye. Imagine that."

After a few minutes' watching and imagining, the couple bid their farewells and walked off toward the victory party being held at the MooseRack.

Across the street, someone else bellowed something about a free victory party lunch at the MooseRack, and the street was instantly filled with cars and pickups and vans and motorcycles.

"Imagine that," Roxy said quietly, and knowingly, studiously watching the same tide Kent watched. "Enough money to provide a free meal for all those people who wanted to rescue us last night."

Kent looked southward along Beachfront, and grinned. "Yes. Imagine that." He shaded his eyes against the bright sunlight. "Now what's he doing?"

Roxy looked. "Who, him?"

Dwight Lepeche was standing at the curb, industriously polishing a blinding white van with a cartoon picture of a cockroach on the side.

Roxy laughed. "I heard he decided not to go back to the

woods. He's going to become an exterminator instead."

Kent made a face. "Cor. Imagine having to work all day with all those smelly chemicals."

"I don't think," she said quietly, "he intends to use chemicals. More of a natural process, he said. Environmentally safe."

Kent opened his mouth, closed it, and hoped the man would be able to watch his weight. Summer, in Maine, was a virtual Riviera for bugs.

"Say," Roxy said then.

He looked at her.

She wouldn't look at him. "Are you going to be in town long?"

He shrugged.

She looked at him sideways. "I never did thank you for saving my life."

Two women strolled long the beach, a man in a yellow slicker between them.

"It's all right," he said modestly. "You did your part. Quite well, I might add."

She blushed.

He grinned.

"Especially the note."

She tried to deny it, shrugged, and said, "I couldn't help it. I had a theory."

A car honked behind them, and they turned.

Professor Tarkingdale leaned out the passenger window and waved. "We're off now," the little man called.

"Now?" Kent muttered, and Roxy slapped his arm.

"When you get back to London," the professor said, "give me a ring, won't you?"

"I suppose you're going to report to your Inner Circle?" Kent said. "And maybe even think about retiring and settling down with Dianna?"

Tarkingdale ducked his head bashfully.

"How did he *know* that?" Dianna yelled from behind the wheel. "Goddamnit, Sloan, ask him how he knew that."

Kent waved.

Tarkingdale waved.

The car sped away.

Kent looked back to the beach, and to the women walking with the man along the wet apron of sand.

"I might," he said, "stay here for a while. Just to make sure it's all . . . over."

"That's nice," Roxy answered noncommitally.

"I mean—"

And he quieted at the sound of an engine puttering up the road.

He turned.

Roxy turned.

A spiffy red motor scooter popped over the curb and skidded to a halt beside him. It was ridden by a man in jeans, western boots, a denim jacket, and a worn but lovable grey western hat. From a saddlebag he pulled a large package which he handed to Kent.

"Be damned," Kent said. "I didn't think you'd be here this time."

The man smiled. "If you don't like it, you can always go back to being a butler."

Kent grinned.

The man tipped his hat to Roxy and puttered swiftly away.

The package was heavy; Kent almost kissed it.

Roxy sighed. Loudly. "Your new movie, I take it?"

"Yep. Think so."

She edged closer. "You gonna open it?"

"Nope. Don't think so. Not now, anyway."

She edged closer. "When?"

When he turned his head, their noses damn near collided. He blinked.

"Damnit, Roxanne," a voice called from the beach. "You stop that public canoodling right now, you hear me? You stop it this instant and get back to the machine. We got a ton of cakes to make by morning."

Kent searched the beach for the source of the scolding, and saw one of the two women, smoking a pipe, standing in the water with her hands on her hips. The other woman, much younger, had her arm around the man in the yellow slicker.

"Roxy," the younger woman called, "he the one with the flaps?"

Kent stiffened.

Roxy tried a laugh. "My mother, Armenia. That's my little sister, Tammie."

"Flaps." he said.

"That's my father they have there. He's dead, you know."

"Flaps."

"Rowena stuffed him, remember?"

Flaps, he thought; good lord, I'll never be able to come back. She'll have that all over town before sunset. I'm going to have to start all over again, find someplace else to go when I want to get away from it all.

He glared at her.

She shrugged.

Her mother yelled again and dragged her husband away from a scavenging band of bandaged terns.

Flaps, he thought miserably.

"Damn," Roxy muttered.

He definitely did not want to ask, but why the hell, he thought, should things change now?

"What."

"A button came off."

He said nothing.

She said nothing.

He refused to look.

Time passed.

She said, "So, is that it?"

He thought for a moment, and nodded.

"We really done?"

He nodded a second time and slipped off the wall.

"We can go now?"

"Yes."

"Damn."

"What now, Roxanne? Another button gone, so that I'll have to make some sort of wiseass man-type remark and you'll have to come back with some kind of sneering woman-type innuendo?"

"Nope. But my jeans are ripped all to hell."

He sighed. He smiled. He plucked her off the wall and began to carry her down the street. It didn't matter that his cottage was a mile and a half away; it didn't matter that she was whispering some rather fishy theories about flaps and hairy cattle in his ear; and it didn't matter that his new script weighed an effing ton.

What mattered was that he was alive, he had a job, and he had the girl.

He looked up at the sky.

So what the hell else did you want from a happy ending? Trumpets?

The concertina played.

Close enough, he thought; close enough.

THE CREDITS

STARRING AS THEMSELVES:

Laurence Ardlaw	Tammie Lott
Rowena Bingham	Roxanne Lott
Belinda Durando	Kent Montana
Marty Ellegra	Buddy Plimsol
Jared Graverly	Cornelia Popper
Freddie Horton	Wilma Popper
Mabel Horton	Eddie Salem
Purity Horton	Claw Tackard
Doc Jones	Sloan Tarkingdale
Frieda Juleworth	Dianna Torne
Dwight Lepeche	Lavinia Volle
Armenia Lott	Lamar de la von Zaguar

SPECIAL APPEARANCES BY:

The Sage But Confused Man .... Peter Cushing
The Confused Not So Sage Man .... Ralph Bates
Script Messenger .... Mysterious Person
And:

BRUNO, THE CANARY OF A THOUSAND FACES

Producer .... Northgate 386/20
Director .... Lionel Fenn
Writer .... Lionel Fenn
Editor .... Ginjer Buchanan
Assistant to Miss Torne .... Rip
Film .... Hammer
Bats .... Joe DiMaggio
Swing Gang .... Benny Goodman Quintet

Lamp Operator	Diogenes
Foley	Red
Hair Dresser	Elvira
Miniatures	Mickey Rooney
^Cliff	Robertson

AND SPECIAL THANKS TO:

Rick Hautala, for all the free books whose stories took place in Maine and didn't tell me a damn thing about it, so it's all his fault; Christopher Lee, for being tall and reuniting Kent with his nanny; the Kent Montana Fan Club, who didn't know Kent had a nanny; and the Department of Fish, Wildlife, and Eateries, Assyria, in Maine, without whose assistance none of the actors would have tasted the exquisite Assyrian blowfish cake, even if they couldn't get the director to eat one on a bet.

Not to mention, but we will anyway, HAGGIS, the official newsletter of the Kent Montana Fan Club, a totally new, cheap but kind of classy publication designed to enhance, complement, and unashamedly shill the Kent Montana/Lionel Fenn filmatic book experience. There are no pretensions here. There are no intellectual assaults upon your vital critical thinking abilities. The newsletter is designed for no other reason than to have some ridiculous fun, tell some truly awful jokes, write really long sentences, and generally mess around with reality a little, a commodity we have, in our opinion, too damn much of these days.

If you're squeamish, $3.00 (U.S.) will get you the latest issue by return mail; if you're bold, daring, and adventurous, $12.00 (U.S.) will get you 5 sort of packed issues (one year). Checks in either amount payable to Kent Montana Fan Club; editorial/subscription address is PO Box 97, Newton, NJ 07860.

No kidding.

No guarantees either, but what the hell.